MW01142822

This book has been donated to

_____

by
Pacific Northwest
Children's Literature Clearinghouse

Authorized signature: _____

SIGNS & WONDERS

SIGNS & WONDERS

Pat Lowery Collins

Houghton Mifflin Company
Boston 1999

The author wishes to thank Lenice Strohmeir,
Suzanne Freeman, and Ellen Wittlinger, who read the
manuscript in progress either in part or in its entirety
and offered encouragement and helpful suggestions.

———◆———

The text of this book is set in 13-point Bembo.

Library of Congress Cataloging-in-Publication Data

Collins, Pat Lowery.
Signs and wonders / Pat Lowery Collins.
p.   cm.
Summary: In a series of letters, a fourteen-year-old convent
school student who never knew her mother and resents her
father, grapples with her belief that God has chosen her to
give birth to a prophet.
ISBN 0-395-97119-5
[1. Parent and child—Fiction. 2. Letters—Fiction.]   I. Title.
PZ7.C69675Si   1999
[Fic]—dc 21   99-10647   CIP

Printed in the United States of America
BP 10 9 8 7 6 5 4 3 2 1

*To Kim, Colleen, and Cathlin,
and all dedicated mothers*

SIGNS & WONDERS

ONE

———◆———

Sunday, September 6

Dear Pim:

I'm writing to you because there isn't anyone else. I intend to write to Mavis, of course, but not the kind of letter I'm writing to you. You remember how she never let me call her any form of "grandmother" because she didn't feel old enough to be one?

I have never told her anything important. She thinks there isn't anything important in the life of a fourteen-year-old girl, or won't be anytime soon. She's wrong, as I'm sure you'd agree: Important things can happen to very young people. Think of Joan of Arc. Think of the Virgin Mary. We are told here to think of her all day long, that she is the Mediatrix of all Graces. I'm not sure what it means, but I like the way it sounds. We say

1

the Angelus, her own prayer, three times a day. As far as I'm concerned, it isn't often enough. Chanting it while the bells chime makes me kind of weak. It starts out, "My Soul doth magnify the Lord." Isn't that amazing?

I was four when you left. Why did you? Do you know that I can remember exactly what you looked like—the misty green suit, a kind of green I've never seen since, your glassy skin. And I still remember the things you told me. "Follow me," you'd say in a voice that sounded like several small flutes playing at once, or "Careful," "Watch out," "Stay away," "Go to sleep."

Mavis always smiled when I saved a seat for you at the table or a place beside my bed. She thought I talked to some imaginary friend, like other children. But I was never like other children. Now that I'm older, I've decided you're probably one of the cherubim, which the encyclopedia says are a lower order of angels. Maybe you're in some order even lower than that because you never did have wings. I expect you're some kind of guardian as well, that I needed you very badly once and that you're still around somewhere, only I'm not allowed to see you anymore. Just in case I need you very badly again, I thought we should stay in touch. Are you surprised to hear from me?

Mavis has sent me here because she's afraid. She's afraid of so many things it's unreal, and even though I know it's because she wants to protect me, it's pretty suffocating. She thinks I'll become wild like my mother, now that I've entered my teens. She still keeps telling me how when my mother left me with her when I was a baby, when she ran away, it broke her heart. I will tell her sometime that a heart that grows up with no mother can also end up in pieces.

I don't really understand why Mavis had to pick a place quite so far away from everything. There isn't even a town you can walk to—or bicycle to for that matter. There's a lake somewhere, though I haven't seen it yet. It's why the school is called "Our Lady of the Lake." There are mountains (I guess we're on top of one) and trees—giant pines that tower above the outside walls. We arrived at night, so I didn't see much. The roads twisted, and we were definitely climbing from the time we left the highway.

It's a very small school. Only twenty girls. Each of us has her own tiny narrow room with high windows. Clara, who helped me get settled, says the rooms are just like the nuns' cells. (She has been here three years and saw one once.) She says she'll probably be a nun because if she is here very much longer, she may not know how to be anything else. Clara says if it weren't for her very positive attitude, it might feel like a prison sometimes—the way there isn't any place to go even if you want to. Most of the new girls already hate it here. I was prepared to, but I don't.

Sister Eduard has just knocked on the door to tell me it's almost time to turn out the lights. It is precisely nine o'clock. I like that. But I still need to write to Mavis. And Charles—maybe.

Your person,

Taswell

Sunday, September 6

Dear Mavis,

I don't know how you found this place! It is very medieval for being in the United States of America at the end of the Twentieth Century. And it must be the last convent on earth where the nuns wear the same style habit as their Belgian foundress. Last night we could hear wolves outside the walls. Grace, one of the novices, the ones studying to be nuns, says they're harmless, that they never really hurt people except in fairy tales. She knows all about them and their packs and says that if humans acted a little more like wolves, we'd be much more civilized.

There are three novices. Grace is the only pretty one. The other two look like nuns already, all scrubbed and pimply. There is one postulant, Edna, who will take her first vows at the end of the year. She dresses all in white and never talks to anyone. It's hard to tell if she is pretty. She's so all-the-same-all-over—her skin, her hair, her dress or robe or whatever it is. Her eyes seem almost washed away.

Just so you know, I wouldn't have gotten into any trouble if you'd let me stay with you and go to regular school, even though you'd be at the office every day or traveling. You wouldn't have had to worry about "bad company," as you call it. I'm used to not having friends. I don't expect to have any here either.

Sister Eduard says there is no saint Taswell. She wonders how I ever got baptized. I was baptized, wasn't I? Please let me know soon. I need to know.

Your loving granddaughter,

Taswell

Sunday, September 6

Dear Charles,

Mavis says your newest wife is very young. How young? Did you ever think she might be marrying you for your money? It happens a lot. You're right, I would not want to live with you. It would be too weird.

Your daughter,

Taswell

TWO

Thursday, September 10

Dear Pim:

We have been on "retreat." They call it "Retreat Week" and it always starts the school year here. Everyone wears veils that look like cheesecloth and we have to be absolutely quiet. You can't even talk at meals, which is all right with me because you get hungry here in the mountains. Sister Bruno makes all kinds of good bread and biscuits and homemade sausage and potatoes with gravy.

I sit at the table for new girls. There are six of us. Sister Eugenie, the Retreat Mistress, keeps shushing Madeline, who can't stop talking no matter what and giggles right through the rosary. Sometimes she's sent into the hall, but when she's allowed back, she just starts talking again. I'm glad we aren't supposed to talk.

I wish this was a permanent rule.

I do have something important to tell you, but it will have to wait. Our Retreat Master, Father Cleanth, says patience is one of the most misunderstood virtues. That we are all waiting for Eternity. The small things we wait for while we're waiting for that, really don't matter very much. In my case, though, what I'm waiting for will matter to a great many people. It overwhelms me when I think about it. I need to pray over it a while longer and take it all in, before I tell you. The temptation is to feel proud. I must remember that I am just an instrument. And *you* must be patient. Come to think of it, you probably already know.

Your person,
Taswell

Thursday, September 10

Dear Mavis,

I thought there might be a letter from you today. You're very busy, I know, but I thought you might have found the time to write since it's my first week away.

Retreat Week has been really quiet. It's something I'm good at—being quiet. You always said I was good at playing by myself. This is like that, like playing alone, only God is listening. Maybe I was autistic in another life. Maybe I liked it.

Your loving granddaughter,
Taswell

Dear Taswell,

Of course you were baptized. What a question! Your middle name is Orelia. It was my sister's name and some saint or other. Tell Sister Eduard that Taswell is a family name. My mother's maiden name actually. But you know that. Why didn't you tell her yourself?

And that other letter! It was very odd. All that talk about silence and autism and another life. You should watch that kind of thing or people will think you are as eccentric as Uncle Jules. But you're not like him. You're a perfectly normal child who needs to be more outgoing. Perhaps Our Lady of the Lake is not the right environment for you (you seem to be going through such an overly religious phase), but I am terribly concerned that you be protected. The world we live in has become a completely unsafe place, even worse than when your mother was young.

You seemed so distracted when we said goodbye that I felt quite bereft, as if you weren't going to miss me at all. Naturally, I didn't think you'd want to hear from me right away.

Please do think about what I've said.

Fondly,

Mavis

P.S. Are you getting enough to eat? Institutional food may not have variety, but I was assured it would be wholesome and locally grown. The nuns check everything thoroughly before it is cooked and have assured me that all meat products would be well done. They have bought their meat from the same butcher for many years. Having no local variety store means that you can't possibly buy tainted candy or over-the-counter medicines that have been tampered with. But you probably don't remember that awful scare over spider eggs in bubble gum and strychnine in Tylenol capsules.

Friday, September 11

Dear Taswell,

Your letter really upset your stepmother and me. In the past your remarks may have been a little peculiar, but never out-and-out rude. Maybe it's all the adjustments you've been asked to make recently. Very reluctantly, I'm going to withhold your allowance until you send an apology.

Perhaps you need more therapy to help you deal with your feelings? Is there any possibility for it in that remote place where Mavis has stashed you away? Is there a school counselor? Please look into this, dear.

Love,
Father

Friday, September 18

Dear Pim,

Two letters in one week! The mail is put at our places at the table. Everyone saw the envelopes.

I've decided that I'll tell you my important stuff in stages. Otherwise, it might be too hard to understand, though if anyone will understand it will be you. I'm prepared for disbelief from others.

People didn't believe Mary when she said she was going to have a baby—God's baby. And she was only fourteen, like me. And she hadn't any husband.

If I had a baby, I wouldn't want to bother with a husband either. I'd want the baby all to myself—a living human who would love me more than anything on earth. Someone that I could hold on to forever and ever.

I saw Edna walking outside the walls yesterday. You would think she'd be afraid of the wolves. She looks like a nurse, all in white, or maybe like a shepherd. Sometimes I see her going up the steps to the tower to ring the bells for the Angelus. She always stares straight ahead. Maybe that's what you do when you're really holy. Do you suppose Mary talked to people or only to angels?

Mary was overshadowed by the Holy Spirit. Did you know that? Isn't that a great word, *overshadowed?* I'll have to look it up.

Your person,
Taswell

Dear Mavis,

You are worried again that I will be anorexic like cousin Pia. I am not like Pia. I'm not afraid of my body. I think you're right that I'll be getting fatter, though. What I'd like is a nice loose shroud. Dark blue maybe instead of these insipid pastel plaid uniforms.

Of course I miss you, Mavis, but I think this is a good place for me right now. I was angry at first. But it has become increasingly clear that I'm supposed to be here.

I wrote to Charles, and he said I was rude about his new bimbette. He wants me to apologize. He wants me back in therapy. He calls her my new stepmother. I never even met the last two, although I guess they didn't actually have a title because he didn't actually marry either one.

Classes are small here, like everything else. I am way ahead in math. We are studying the American Revolution. I did that in sixth grade. In English we are reading Emily Dickinson. Sister Edwina says she was something of a recluse. What is the plural for recluse? Emily never had any children, just poems. Isn't that sad? Is Emily a saint's name?

Today, Grace was watching migrating hawks with binoculars. There were so many and they were so close, I could see them with my bare eyes. She said there were Broad Wings and some Cooper's hawks, that this is their flyway. The nuns have actually helped to preserve it by planting original grasses and wildflowers and doing things to keep the lake alive. It had started to dry up once. It seems like a very holy endeavor, preserving the earth for others. I see them sometimes, working out there in the wind and the sun, like graceful sharecroppers or peasants in one of your Millet paintings.

Your loving granddaughter,

Taswell

Sunday, September 20

Dear Charles,

I apologize. Did you know that there are some things money can't buy? Like therapy on a remote mountain top.

I like it here. It is just strange and boring enough. Did I mention the wolves?

Your daughter,

Taswell

THREE

Sunday, September 27

Dear Pim,

It has been more than an entire week since I last wrote to you. From now on, I'm going to do it more often. I'll need your support. In case you haven't guessed already, Pim, or weren't in on it from the beginning, it's time I tried to explain. It won't be easy.

Remember Family Vespers that first afternoon that I arrived here and how I was praying so hard that Mavis would change her mind and take me back with her? I knew she was looking at me out of the corner of her eye to see if I was crying, but I had already decided I wasn't going to. If she could really do this to me, I wasn't going to give her the satisfaction.

Anyway, in spite of my still being mad at her, the place

was beginning to get to me—the glowing windows, the plainsong, the incense at Benediction. I was starting to feel safe. And something else. One minute I wanted to shout at Mavis; the next, there was this feeling of complete peace, like I knew I belonged here, that I'd been sent here for a purpose. It was so weird. Now I realize it must have been the Holy Spirit preparing me.

And then there was that day, *the day,* during Retreat Week when Father Cleanth was talking about the New Millennium, how we're living in a time of great moment (which the dictionary defines as "of particular importance") and possibility, how prophets often appear at such times, how our troubled planet needs a prophet more than ever before. This time, he said, the prophet might, in fact, be a woman.

At first I thought he was just saying that about a woman because of this being a school for girls, but then I got the incredible thought, "Why not?" as though someone had planted a clump of roots in my head and they immediately started to stretch out and grow, and little jerking lights started up inside my eyes. Everywhere I looked there was a circle of them. Then the circle began to grow until I couldn't see anything but the lights. I couldn't read the hymns when we stood to sing. The pages seemed sucked blank in the middle. When even the words around the edges were gone, the lights disappeared; I could see normally, but I had the worst headache of my entire life.

In the infirmary, Sister Brigid told me I probably had a migraine, that migraines sometimes start visually like that. But I've never had one before. More and more, I'm becoming certain that it was some kind of sign.

By now you're probably thinking that I expect to be this prophet. But I would never ever be that presumptuous. (Presumption is a sin. Did you know that?) As I think I said before, what finally became clear to me, and what I really expect, is to be an instrument, the means by which the prophet will come into the world. How does that grab you?

There are accounts of other virgin births besides Mary's, you know. I wonder—if God does decide to choose me as an instrument to bring forth a prophet for the New Millennium, will I be overshadowed by an archangel, maybe, or a saint? Will I know it?

Your person,
Taswell

Tuesday, October 6

Dear Taswell,

Why do you insist on being rude to your father? It was your mother, after all, who abandoned you. To his credit, he has tried to be there for you whenever possible. And being from a family of means, he has never been stingy with support payments. I do resent his suggesting therapy again unless he plans to pay for it. I can barely afford the tuition. Yes, he was willing to pay at

Trimble. But he's totally opposed to Our Lady's, and as I am your legal guardian, I won't have him dictating the terms and place of your schooling. At any rate, try not to antagonize him.

And what's this new obsession with saints' names?

I'm glad the food is all right, if a bit on the starchy side. It may fatten you up.

And this talk about shrouds. You are continually trying to shock me.

Fondly,

Mavis

Saturday, October 10

Dear Pim,

There have been no new signs. I consider this a major opportunity to practice the virtue of patience.

Today the novices took everyone to the lake in the two school vans. They are terrible drivers, and it turned out that we could easily have walked—or climbed—down there. One thing you definitely don't get around here is exercise. There is something called "gymnasium sports" twice a week, where we try to hit a medicine ball across a volleyball net or we jump around on a trampoline. There is one outdoor tennis court, but it's cracked and overgrown with weeds, and the swimming pool is behind a fence, with only a little green rainwater in the bottom and a rusty mess of leaves.

I have to admit, the lake is beautiful. Mavis would say "breathtaking." The trees dip gold and red branches over it in places. The far banks seem on fire. Today the water was the color of the sky.

Madeline and the other new girls giggled and played hide-and-seek like children. (I'm convinced now that most of the girls are sent here because they're behavior problems.) They've learned that I don't like that sort of thing. I jogged on the path alongside of Grace, who pointed out some of the different kinds of moss and lichen. It was quite interesting. Grace at least knows enough not to ask personal questions.

Do you know anything about what I told you before? Have you been supernaturally informed in any way?

Your person,

Taswell

Tuesday, October 6

Dear Taswell,

If your exceedingly brief description is at all accurate, I'm even more opposed to the school Mavis has chosen than at the outset. It sounds like something out of another century. Girls your age need to mix with both genders on a daily basis. To my mind, single-gender schools are archaic. I will do my best to convince her of her mistake. You should be going to parties, falling in love.

In the meantime, what would you say to a few weeks in Switzerland for a ski vacation? Monique is an expert and would be happy to teach you. We could stay at a small pension I know in St. Moritz. Let me know when you expect to have winter break.

Love,

Father

Friday, October 16

Dear Pim,

Still no signs. I'm getting worried. If you know anything at all, I wish you'd tell me somehow.

Your person,

Taswell

Monday, October 12

Dear Taswell,

Your dad says he's invited you to ski with us in midwinter. I'm so excited about it! He talks about you all the time, and this would give us a chance to really get acquainted. He's so proud of how well you already ski, but says you might want to learn some of the finer points, which I'd be happy to teach you.

I really hope you'll come.

Love,

Monique

Dear Pim,

Can you imagine! Monique has written to me, and we haven't even been introduced. I don't know why she thinks she has to impress me. She's already married to my father.

The little skiing trip they have planned couldn't come at a worse time. And if I wanted a friend, I definitely wouldn't pick her. Did you know that Charles was a family friend of Mavis's before he seduced my mother? Apparently he has always liked younger women. Mother ran away before they could marry. I am a bastard. Mavis told me all this. The dictionary defines *bastard* as "An illegitimate child" or "Something that is of irregular, inferior, or dubious origin." I'm not even supposed to be here.

But I am.

Your person,

Taswell

Dear Mavis,

I haven't heard from you in a while. Father has written. And the Bimbette. Isn't that strange? She wants to be my friend. That is even stranger.

I expect you are busy putting together the new list or having lunch with authors. Will the BEA be meeting in Chicago again? Maybe you can visit me on the way. Since it isn't until June, maybe you'll have another trip somewhere close by before then. Can I come home for Thanksgiving? What about Christmas?

Grace has been teaching our religion class. She knows a lot about the lives of the saints. We use the textbook that your friend Daniel wrote. It's the new edition and includes the North American Martyrs. Grace does not like people very much. You can tell. Except historical ones. She loves them. And she loves everything in the natural world. I understand how she feels. I even like her for it. I think that's what Sister Edwina would call ironic.

The nuns put on street clothes when they leave to get supplies or attend conferences and things. I can't imagine why they'd want to. It makes them look so ordinary, like completely different people.

Don't worry about the shroud.

Your loving granddaughter,

Taswell

Monday, October 26

Dear Pim,

We had dance class today instead of gymnasium sports. Sister Kathleen is going to teach us Irish Step Dancing after we have a unit of modern dance. She demonstrated in her habit, which she had to scrunch up over her thighs. Her ankles are thick as posts. I liked the very controlled kicks and turns, the way your whole upper body turns to stone.

Modern dance, on the other hand, looks pretty silly, with everyone flopping around in her own little world. I got dizzy and had to sit down.

Do you ever watch any of this stuff or are there other places you have to be?

It has recently occurred to me that I may not be holy enough, or that maybe, because of my irregular origin, God will pick Edna, though it would certainly interfere with her plans to be a contemplative. Grace doesn't like children. The other two novices, Sylvia and Dorine, can barely take care of themselves and are constantly late to chapel. It could be a student other than me, I suppose, but there clearly aren't any as responsible as I am.

I continue to wait for a sign and to practice the virtue of patience.

Your person,
Taswell

Monday, October 26

Dear Mavis,

It is almost November, and you haven't said anything about my coming home for Thanksgiving. Please let me know so I can tell Sister Veronica in the office. She is very particular about having enough notice for things like departures.

I got very dizzy in modern dance a few days ago and haven't felt very well since. Sister Brigid thinks it is a low grade infection of some kind. They gave me a day off from classes and Sister Bruno's chicken soup. (She could slip something into the soup, you know, without too much trouble. Just kidding. Though it tasted kind of funny and made me awfully sleepy.) I think I might feel better if I could come home for a few days.

Please write soon about the holidays.

Your loving granddaughter,

Taswell

Wednesday, October 21

Dear Taswell,

Monique is waiting for your reply. I think you should know that it was very brave of her to write to you, given your attitude. She is really quite a shy person. I tell you this because I don't want to see her hurt. She is sincere in wanting to be your friend. It would make it so much easier all the way around.

I hope that school isn't as much of a prison as it sounds. A girl your age should be having fun and the freedom to try new things. Perhaps your mother wouldn't have bolted if Mavis hadn't been so controlling. Well—we'll never know. She seems to have completely disappeared. I have forgotten her face.

Love,

Father

Dear Pim,

Of course Charles has forgotten my mother's face. There have been so many women since. What can possibly be so special about the newest one. Shy? Let's get real. She and I have nothing to say to each other and never will.

There is going to be a Halloween party. Isn't that childish? And we're supposed to wear costumes. Since it's like an order, I'm going to have to think of something. A hawk, I think, with beautiful wings. I'm going to make a really big beak and peck out Madeline's eyes. That should be fun. In Art once we made masks out of papier mâché. I'll see if there's any more in the art department and probably make the wings out of cardboard. There isn't much to work with here.

I threw up twice last week, early in the morning. Sister Brigid thinks I still have that infection in my system. It must be why I'm not hungry except at dinner.

Your person,
Taswell

Monday, November 1

Dear Taswell,

Sister Eduard called to tell me that you created quite a scene at the Halloween party. The girl you attacked in your hawk suit apparently became hysterical, and it ruined the party for everyone. I'm very disturbed about this and can't imagine why you would perform such a hostile act, especially since all your letters indicate that you are happy there.

Sister Eduard also says that you have made no friends and only converse with the nuns or the novices. I know you warned me of this, but I thought you were attempting to shock me again. She says that since you have been feeling so queasy, she plans to call the local internist in to give you a thorough checkup. If you continue to be so antisocial, the matter of another therapist will have to be approached as well (just as your father has suggested to me). What is this about your spending an inordinate amount of time in chapel? *Hours* at a time is how Sister Eduard described it. I can't help wondering why you're given such unsupervised opportunities.

I will be in Frankfurt over Thanksgiving. It can't be helped. Sister Bruno will no doubt make a magnificent feast, and I'm sure there will be other girls remaining there. It's such a short holiday, after all, hardly time to drive back and forth from anywhere. You would be less lonely if you made a friend or two. Please try.

Fondly,
Mavis

Dear Mavis,

The thing about the party wasn't as big a deal as Sister Eduard made it out to be. The girls here are infantile. And as fragile as glass. Normal people wouldn't have been upset at all.

And I don't need to see a doctor, Mavis, *or* a therapist. I'm feeling better.

I was looking forward to Thanksgiving. Short holidays can be nice, too, you know. Remember when Emil would drive us into Manhattan and you and I would have Thanksgiving together at Rumpelmeyers, the waiters hovering all around us like fat elves. I loved that and didn't even mind that you never wanted to go to the Macy's Parade. Well, Christmas isn't so far away.

Your loving granddaughter,

Taswell

Thursday, November 5

Dear Pim:

I just lied to Mavis about feeling better. At least I don't feel worse. I feel like a dope, though, for not catching on sooner. I suddenly remembered the time when Mavis's secretary, Carol, was sick for a couple of months with what everybody said was the Asian flu. I guess I was supposed to be too young to understand, and no one came right out and explained it, but it didn't take much for a ten-year-old to make the connection between her mysterious sick spell and the baby that arrived about six months later.

What I don't understand, though, is when did it happen to me, this overshadowing or whatever? And why wasn't there some declaration? Why didn't I get a chance to agree or say something memorable, the way Mary did? Make up a prayer, maybe. Oh, well. What really matters is that I've been chosen, just the way I knew I would be. So what if it wasn't very grand! God works in mysterious ways. Right?

Now—it's so wonderful—I'm never alone. There is this tiny heart right beneath mine. It beats so fast. I hear it even when I sleep.

Your person,

Taswell

Saturday, November 7

Dear Charles,

I don't feel like a trip right now or like meeting new people and making new friends. Mavis has probably told you that I'm having some problems adjusting. I think she's exaggerating, but it's probably a good idea not to complicate things by leaving this place and going to some foreign country. I like it here in spite of everything.

Your daughter,

Taswell

Dear Pim,

Mavis isn't going to come and get me, even for a few days. It figures. She's so big on holidays, decorating the house like a department store, but I can always tell she can't wait to get back to her work.

Maybe it's just as well, though. She might notice that I'm not myself. It's easier to pretend around the nuns. And the other girls have left me pretty much alone since Halloween. If they only knew how I've been singled out. But they are so emotionally retarded.

Grace did ask me why I chose to imitate the predatory characteristics of the hawk when I could have so easily emulated its grace and majesty. I think it was a very good question, and I regret now that I gave in to such petty theatrics. Given my condition, it was, in fact, very inappropriate behavior. My anger must be directed where it belongs and not at my immature peers. Where does it belong, Pim? I'm not always sure.

I am memorizing Emily Dickinson's poems. Do you know the one about the bee? The part that goes "His labor is a chant/His idleness a tune." I feel like the bee sometimes. Especially now. And I'm making up prayers. "My soul is like a bird of the air. I place myself in the downdrafts of the Lord." What do you think?

If I were a bird, where would I fly? I know I'd build

a nest in the absolutely tallest tree so I could look at God.

Your person,
Taswell

Dear Taswell,

Monique and I are disappointed that you don't want to come and see us right now, of course. But as it turns out, she won't be skiing this winter, after all, for we're expecting a baby. Isn't that fantastic! And this time the child will have a real family that includes you. Can you find it in your heart to welcome a new brother or sister, dear?

Monique sends her love. She hasn't been feeling too well, but the doctor says she's doing just fine.

Love,
Father

Wednesday, November 18

Dear Mavis,

Isn't it disgusting! Charles and Monique are expecting a baby. He's old enough to be its grandfather. And they think I should be pleased. Me! The Foundling! You must be as angry as I am.

Well, Happy Thanksgiving and Bon Voyage or whatever.

Your loving granddaughter,
Taswell

Monday, November 23

Dear Taswell,

How hostile you've become! And, no, I do not share your feelings about the coming blessed event. Monique is young and probably wants children of her own very much. And your father was never a bad parent, just an absent one. Perhaps he will do better this time. I'm sure they want to include you in their happiness. This baby might indeed be the needed link between you and your dad. Won't you try to open up a little and take that enormous chip off your shoulder?

I leave for Frankfurt on Tuesday. You'll find my itinerary enclosed, with numbers where I can be reached. I'll call on Wednesday instead of the holiday as it will be much easier to get through. Just in case we don't connect, have a very pleasant Thanksgiving. I will indeed be thinking of you.

Fondly,
Mavis

Saturday, November 28

Dear Pim,

Why am I feeling so depressed? With my secret knowledge, I should feel the peace of great privilege. But how I wish I could announce my pregnancy just like Monique. This, too, however, is clearly a test of my patience and perseverance. All the fuss will be made over her, and I will have to await the great event in silence.

I wish there was something in the library here that would tell about all the physical stuff, about what to expect. We did have that one unit of Marriage and the Family in seventh grade, but I wasn't too interested in those pictures of the baby being born. But then, Mary couldn't have known much, either. And Joseph almost didn't marry her when he found out about the baby. He had a message from an angel, though. And so did she, for that matter. I sure would like some outside help like that. Don't you, don't the lesser orders, have any influence at all? Right now, all I've got is faith, and it's probably not as much as you get when you're a saint.

It's become hard to close the top snap on my jeans and button the top buttons on these ridiculous plaid skirts.

Sister Eduard is having that internist examine me tomorrow because she says I still look peaked. I won't be able to tell him the truth. I will have to act like I feel fine.

A baby's heartbeat is very, very fast. Like a runaway clock.

Your person,
Taswell

FOUR

Dear Mavis,

I thought you liked it the way it is now—you and me. We're a family, too, you know. Why would I want to be part of some other family? And when my real mother comes back, I want to be there. She isn't going to go back to Charles. She can't. But she might come back to us.

I am actually sort of interested in Monique's baby, though. Could you maybe send me a paperback book or something about how babies get born and everything. I'm just curious.

I really miss you. I wanted to talk to you, but I guess your call never got through or no one gave me the message. They're terrible, here, about giving messages.

Your loving granddaughter,

Taswell

Dear Charles and Monique,

Mavis says I should be happy for you. So congratulations.

Since it will be my first half sister or half brother, I have no special feelings in the matter. But I'm sure you do.

Your daughter,
Taswell

Dear Pim,

The doctor turned out to be a woman, but I was still really nervous when she (when Dr. Philips) examined me. When she wanted to know the date of my last period I just made something up. I wasn't about to tell her I haven't had one since I've been here. And when she asked if I had a boyfriend and had I been sexually active before coming to Our Lady's, it made me think she must suspect something. It took me quite a while to realize that she has a whole ready-made string of questions and doesn't expect yes answers to them from the socially immature types that go to school here, myself included.

Grace is driving me into town for some routine blood tests tomorrow. Dr. Philips says she thinks I'm just a little run down, anemic maybe, and the nausea could be because of the higher altitudes. Altitude sickness she calls it.

Mavis FedExed me a huge hardcover book on birthing customs around the world that she edited a few years ago. Apparently she really doesn't want me to know too many details, just all these weird customs. I mean, I'm hardly going to invite everyone in the "village" to participate, like the Samoans, or go off from the tribe into some distant field by myself. In these really vague pictures, there seems to be a whole lot of squatting going on. (I just don't believe someone like the Virgin Mary had to worry about that.) Monique will probably have an entire suite in some pristine Swiss hospital.

Grace and I stopped for Mud Slides (hot fudge sundaes in case you don't know) on the way back from town. Mine really tasted great, and I didn't feel so yucky before or even after. I could have eaten two.

Grace told me about her dogs—the ones she had to leave behind with her aunt when she entered the novitiate. She said that was the hardest part. Her mother wouldn't take care of them because she's allergic, and even her aunt keeps complaining. They're golden retrievers, two of them, and she actually talks to them on the phone. She says she knows right away if something's wrong by the tone of their whining and barks.

I don't think I could do that, leave something behind that I'd been taking care of. I mean, I sometimes miss

Mavis's terrier, Bemis, but he always slept at the foot of her bed and was never really mine. Grace says her Calling gave her no choice. Maybe my mother had some kind of calling. I've thought about it, and I think even if she did, she had a choice.

Grace talks a lot about detachment. She says she struggles with it all the time. I'm not sure I know what it is exactly.

Your person,
Taswell

Tuesday, December 8

Dear Taswell,

The doctor's report was a great relief to me. The slight anemia can be easily corrected, and I'm glad she's insisting that you take vitamin pills in addition to the iron. You should be feeling much better in no time and perhaps have a more positive attitude again.

The book fair in Frankfurt was exhausting and there has been absolutely no time to get my bearings before the big promotional push for our new nature series. Right before Christmas if you can believe it! We will manage to have the holiday together, though I hope you'll understand if I need to work through much of your vacation. I'm sending Emil to pick you up on the Thursday after next. I just can't take the day off to drive back and forth with him. Think of things that we can

do together when you get here that won't take too
much time.

Fondly,
Mavis

Saturday, December 5

Dear Taswell,

Quite suddenly, it looks as though business concerns
will bring me to New York over Christmas. Monique
says she's feeling well enough, now, to come along. So
even if it isn't exactly a vacation in the Swiss Alps, we'll
all be able to spend some time together. Mavis has invited us to join you both at her apartment. Monique has
no close living relatives, so this will be a great treat for
her as well as a way of getting you two together at last.

Love,
Father

Saturday, December 12

Dear Pim:

Yuck! Thanksgiving was no fun at all and now
Christmas will be ruined, too. Any time Mavis could
spend with me will be wiped out by the presence of
Charles and his pregnant consort. Why didn't anyone
check with me? I'd just stay here, if most of the nuns
weren't going home, too. Grace is going directly to her
aunt's house to see her dogs. She says even Clara and

Edna have families of their own to visit, though it's hard to believe. I'll bet Madeline's family can't wait to have her nonstop drivel all over their house again.

I looked up *detachment* in the dictionary. One of the meanings is "indifference to or remoteness from the concerns of others." It's just about what I thought it was and perfect for what I need. Now, in addition to practicing patience, I'll definitely need to practice detachment. Actually, I think I've been doing it right along, so it shouldn't be too hard—a great opportunity really, to practice it with Charles and Monique. Even if it's not a virtue exactly, it must be something good, or Grace wouldn't be so bent out of shape about it.

There was a Christmas ornament—a tiny wooden crèche—on my desk when I came back from dinner, right between two notebooks, where I didn't see it right away. You put it there, didn't you? It's a sign, isn't it? Finally! I was beginning to think you had no connections at all. I'll take it home for Mavis's tree, and even though I can't tell any of them yet, seeing it there, I won't feel quite so bottled up and alone with this. Thanks, Pim.

Your person,
Taswell

FIVE

Thursday, December 17

Dear Pim:

It was incredibly boring, driving home with Emil! He always acts like I must be just dying to know about his daughter's latest boyfriends. She sounds like an incredible airhead. The conversation was just a longer version of the short one-sided ones we used to have when he drove me back and forth to school.

The apartment looks just the same. Beatrice still vacuums up crumbs and dust before they even fall to the carpet. I never noticed it before, but the entry hall is like the vestibule of a church. And there's still that wonderful old smell coming from all the ancient furniture and Mavis's collection of antique prints. I wonder how it lingers when everything is so absolutely clean.

Mavis wasn't here when I arrived, so I sat by myself in the library, drinking hot chocolate that Beatrice made and watching the boats going up and down the Hudson. It was good to be alone in this room again, to try to connect with who I was before. It's just been a few months, but I'm not the same at all, and if I'm going to be leaving things I love behind, I want to get close to them again, experience some of the old feelings.

Beatrice says I've "plumped up." She obviously thinks it's a good thing, but of course, she hasn't a clue.

Mavis surprised me by coming home early. When I looked up from the window, there she was—so beautiful for someone almost sixty, her small soft body framed by the doorway, her long silver hair caught back with silver clips. I wish Mavis could know my secret by just looking at me, the way St. Anne did when Mary visited, so that I'd never have to come right out and tell her. But, of course, she isn't anything like St. Anne. The skirt she was wearing was shorter than some of mine, and I could smell her perfume from clear across the room.

Beatrice says my mother looks exactly like Mavis, only younger and darker. I wish I looked even a little bit like them. But, as Mavis says, I'm rawboned and tall like my father. I'm not really sure if he's handsome. The women must think so. Mavis says I have his eyes, which are green and clear as the aggies in his marble collection but with huge dark pupils swimming inside. I know

I'm practically blind like him without my glasses. His hair is dark like mine, too, but where it used to be really thick, the last time I saw him there was a round bald spot on the top, like a shiny island. I wonder if that will ever happen to me.

As I'm writing this in my room, there's a commotion downstairs of people arriving. I don't want to see anyone else, yet, so I'll turn out the light and pretend to be asleep.

Your person,

Taswell

Friday, December 18

Dear Pim,

With everyone suddenly all in one place, there's no one to write to but you. Maybe I'll write to Grace when there's something to tell her. That was Charles and Monique dropping by the other night. Charles tiptoed in and kissed me on the top of my head as if I were a sleeping baby. They came back the next day— rushing in like they couldn't wait to see me. It was all pretty ridiculous.

Monique isn't anything like I thought she'd be, which was small and dark and French. Well, she is French, but she speaks English with almost no accent, and she's even taller than I am. I actually have to look up at her. And she's so—solid. You know, really strong and muscular, as if she works out all the time, with these freckles even on her arms and this really, really red hair that she wears in sort of a tied up bush. I'll bet she played basketball in college, but I'm not going to ask her and give her something to brag about. And she smiles like all the time. It's really weird. I mean, it looks as if she means it, as if she really likes me. But, of course, I'm not buying that.

"I need your help in picking out maternity clothes," she says when we've hardly even said two other words to each other, and she certainly doesn't have any reason to think I know or care anything about the subject. Get a sack, I want to tell her. Get a great big stretchable sack.

Mavis thinks she's "charming." Well, why wouldn't she when she's so unbelievably cheerful. And—get this—she looks at Charles with these dewy bright eyes as if he's the President. And he's just so ordinary looking—exactly the way I remember—and balding even more than last time. And old. He was at least forty when I was born.

How can people think we look anything alike? He has a short beard and is so thin and tall, you expect him to snap in two when he sits down, which he doesn't do very often. He strides around in these flashy running suits as if he's taking a break from a marathon or something. He used to smoke a pipe before Monique got pregnant, and his beard still has a yellow tinge from it around the mouth. The pipe made him look more distinguished. Now he doesn't seem to know what to do with his hands and is always tearing open these little bags of peanuts or scratching his nose. He's so careful with Monique. Treats her as if she's one of Mavis's porcelain figurines. "Sit here, dear," "Don't lift that, dear," "Rest now, dear," "Taswell can do that for you, dear." It's sickening!

Your person,
Taswell

Saturday, December 19

Dear Grace,

I hope your dogs are okay. They are probably very glad to see you.

My new stepmother is tall and athletic looking—sort of like Sister Kathleen only with really red hair and normal ankles.

I'm trying hard to detach from her and my father and pretend it's just me and Mavis, but it isn't easy. They aren't staying here, thank heaven. Charles has meetings in some hotel in Manhattan, so they're sleeping there.

"I'll bet driving back and forth across the river is a real drag," I say. But Monique says, "Oh, no. I just love seeing all the boats and watching the river twist away." She actually said that—twist away. Absolutely everything seems to make her happy, so at least I won't have to go out of my way to please her (which I hadn't planned to do anyway).

I keep telling myself it's only for a week or so, the way you said. I wish you were here to sort of direct me in the detachment stuff, though. Are you not supposed to feel anything at all or what? I mean, I still feel something. Mostly anger. And sometimes, when I think about the future, fear. It looks kind of silly when I write it down. I really don't have anything to be afraid of. I can almost hear you telling me I need to work on the virtue of trust. Right?

How have you come so far with all of this? I mean, how did you get to the place where you could leave something you love behind?

Tonight Mavis and I are eating at Palermos, a little Italian restaurant just down the street that's the best. Charles and Monique are at a banquet or something. There won't be anyone or anything to distract Mavis— no phones, not even Bemis, her dog.

Christmas Day, everyone will be here for dinner. I'm going to midnight mass on Christmas Eve, even if I have to go alone. Actually, I'd rather go alone. It will be easier to meditate.

I haven't had time to Christmas shop and I'm sort of against giving in to material excess, so I'm just sending you some things I found in the card shop down the street. The red ribbons are for your dogs. The holly is for your hair. Almost-nuns can wear things in their hair, can't they?

Your friend,

Taswell

Dear Pim,

It's beginning to feel like I never left here at all, like Our Lady of the Lake is someplace I slipped in and out of in a dream. My room is the same, same bed and blue flowered duvet, same squishy pillows, same posters of the Olympics and of Calvin & Hobbes. My miniature box collection is dusted, but each box is in the same place. Mavis is the same.

The only thing different is having Charles and Monique around. They are so all over each other that I'm glad they won't be here at night. I mean, it would be really embarrassing hearing them, you know, making love in the next room. Monique is so kind of earthy about everything, saying right out loud how she already has to wear nursing bras. Come to think of it, she looks a little like some of those women in the book Mavis sent me who give birth in fields and places, just like animals. I suppose it is all quite natural and everything, and a pregnant virgin is bound to be different and looked on with suspicion. It means I must continue to

43

make every effort to contain my secret, even though I'm sleepy all the time and need to take long naps while Mavis is at work.

When I wake up, curled on my side in my own bed with everything so familiar, I sometimes forget that I'm so totally altered. Beatrice is the only one who notices anything. She says, "You must have got all wore out at that fancy school, poor thing." I think she misses me more than Mavis does.

I got a little confused writing to Grace the other day and said some things really meant for you. Like that fear thing. I probably shouldn't have said that. And I really shouldn't be afraid, being so privileged and everything. Christmas is going to seem weird, though, knowing what I do. Like a rehearsal.

I wonder if Mary thought about, you know, the practical side of things, like where the baby would be born. It doesn't seem she could have. I sure can't think that far ahead yet.

Dinner at Palermos was a little like the Inquisition. Mavis wanted to know all about each and every nun, my grades, my "friends." She hadn't forgotten about the Halloween thing, calling it "not at all consistent with your breeding." I wanted to say that's what you get for breeding someone of "dubious origin," but didn't want to upset her any more than I already have. I tried to tell her how I've outgrown that kind of behavior, but she acts like I'm some powder keg waiting to blow, like I'm getting ready to embarrass her in front of Monique and Charles. But that, as you already know, is not part of my plan. Actually, for once, I don't have a plan. I'm putting everything in God's hands, just the way Grace does. It's not easy to do, you know. As soon as I let go, I want to grab it all back.

Your person,
Taswell

Friday, December 25

Merry Christmas, Pim:

I'm writing this right after midnight mass. Mavis wouldn't let me go alone, even though the church is just two blocks away. So Monique insisted on walking with me, but I made it clear she wasn't welcome. She said she always goes to midnight mass on Christmas Eve. Yeah. Right!

Anyway, there we were, up in front because we got there so early, in time to hear the choir go flat at the end of every single carol. It was hard to meditate with my mother's replacement right there by my elbow. And when I tried to concentrate on the large nativity scene at the base of the altar, I couldn't help thinking how strange it was—both Monique and me carrying babies, me knowing about hers and her not knowing about mine. And how the babies are just sleeping away, not knowing anything at all about their own separate futures. I mean, if they can be so trusting, why can't I?

At the sign of peace, Monique gave me a big hug. I felt really conspicuous, like everyone must be staring. I'm not used to hugs and wouldn't know how to hug back even if I wanted to. It's hard trying to be detached from someone when they hug you like that though.

Walking home, I tried not talking to her. But she kept up the conversation all by herself, telling me about how her family used to celebrate Christmas and about how much she misses her mother and father, who died just a few years ago—one in an accident and the other, she thinks, from grief. It was the first time I'd heard anything about it. I guess she wouldn't make up a thing like that, even if she were trying to make me think she knows how someone feels who has no mother.

"I'm sorry about your mother and father," I told her, "but losing a parent when you're a grownup is not the same as growing up with no mother at all."

"I'm sure you're right," she said. "It's probably worse."

She was really making me mad. "How can it possibly be worse?" I asked.

"Well, I knew and loved my mom," she said. "That's why I miss her so much. You never knew yours, so all you really miss is an idea."

The last part made me so angry I actually stammered, just the way Sister Winifred does all the time.

"That's just it!" I finally got out. "I didn't get to have any of those things, all the things that you miss." I couldn't think right away what they would be.

"Like her guidance and her love and her way of looking at things?" she asked, real unruffled.

"Yeah. Things like that," I said. I was so, kind of embarrassed. I'm not sure why.

"I see what you mean," she said. "Maybe not ever having any of those things *is* worse than having them and then losing them."

I couldn't believe she was agreeing with me.

"You don't need to placate me," I said. "It's pretty clear you're just trying to get on my good side."

And it definitely seemed like I should be given more sympathy because of me being a kid and her being all grown-up with a husband. If she really knew what was going on with me, I wonder what she'd think.

"Oh, and do you have a good side?" she said in the same casual way she says everything. "You've been doing a wonderful job of keeping it hidden."

"It's clear you don't know a thing about detachment," I said then.

"Is that another word for snotty and arrogant?" she wanted to know. This really amazed me since I'd been trying so hard to be—well, not nice, maybe—but neutral.

I snapped back that she probably wouldn't talk to me

like that in front of my father. And do you know what she said then?

"If the subject came up in front of him, I'd say exactly what I'm saying to you now. I'm the same person all the time, you see, not some chameleon unsure of the color of her own skin."

I don't know why, but I started to cry then, sudden hot sobs like when I was a little kid. It really made me mad when Monique just kept walking. I don't know what else I thought she'd do.

When we got back to the apartment, Charles kissed her long and hard, as if she'd been away for weeks. She kind of leaned into him like he was some part of herself she'd left behind. I ran to my room so Charles wouldn't see I'd been crying and so I wouldn't have to witness the way they purr at each other, the way he sometimes seems as pregnant as she is.

Just now, I took the little ornament you gave me off the tree and put it on the table by my bed to remind me of everything, just in case I begin to forget.

Your person,
Taswell

Sunday, December 27

Dear Grace,

Thanks for the calendar of saints' days. Every day now I pray to the saint for that particular one. And keeping a calendar makes me more aware of time passing. It sometimes seems to drag. Other times, things are over before I'm ready, like Christmas. We opened our presents in the morning and then Beatrice made this big phenomenal brunch before going home to her own family. There was the stollen that Mavis likes and my favorite cheese blintzes and a chocolate soufflé and three kinds of omelettes and a honey ham and her special walnut loaf.

In a pact I made with myself, I didn't ask for any gifts this year. Charles and Monique gave me money because they said they don't know my tastes yet, "which will probably be changing." Money from Charles is nice and impersonal and suits me just fine. Mavis gave me a leather jacket which is beautiful but zips up the front and will probably be too tight soon. I gave everyone magazine subscriptions: *National Geographic* for Charles, *Antiques World* for Mavis, and *Playgirl* for Monique. When Mavis saw Monique's, she gave me her drop-dead-on-the-spot look. But, wouldn't you know, Monique said she loved it. Acted as if I'd been serious and it was perfect. Said she'd been reading too much about babies and decorating and things and needed a change. If I gave her a dead rat she'd probably smile and thank me. I don't know what's wrong with her.

I'm beginning to want to go back to Our Lady's. It's

like I need that world to close back around me again, like I belong more there than here right now. Is that what your Calling makes you feel? Not that I have one or anything. But I'm losing track of things here, of myself and what's important.

Be seeing you soon.

Your friend,

Taswell

Sunday, December 27

Dear Pim,

Thought you might want to know about Christmas Day here, in case you had to be someplace else, like around the Throne of God.

Mavis made goose for dinner with her famous chestnut stuffing, and we all helped since Beatrice was at her own house. I kept seeing those beautiful wild geese flying in formation over the lake and wasn't too hungry until the pecan pie. Monique insisted on doing the dishes and Charles helped her. It's the first time I've ever seen him do anything like that. He joked around and juggled plates and things, as if it was some big game. He even snapped the dishtowel at Monique, like a little kid.

Mavis and I sat in front of the fire with Bemis, like guests. It was weird but nice. We talked about what we could see in the flames and about other Christmases.

We wondered where my mother might be now. Mavis says she has trouble picturing her growing older. She wonders if she'd recognize her if they met. She cried some. But I didn't. Monique is right about that anyway. It's hard to cry about someone you never knew.

Charles came in and spoiled everything by plunking down next to Mavis and asking me all kinds of questions, as if I'd want to tell him anything about anything. He tries so hard, but when I didn't get all chatty, he got really bright eyed and asked, "Isn't Monique just great! Isn't she all I said?"

I couldn't remember much of what he'd said, but she sure isn't anything like my former image of her.

"She's very nice," I said. (And I don't know why I should trust either of you, I wanted to add. You're not exactly a real part of my life, you know.) I wonder if he loved my mother as much. I wonder what it would be like to be loved like that.

Your person,

Taswell

SIX

Friday, January 1

Dear Pim,

Happy New Year. Usually I make all sorts of resolutions. But this year will be different. Everything important is already set in motion. I just need to watch it unfold. I still need to work on the virtues of patience and trust. I didn't do so well with detachment over the holidays, but I'm not discouraged. Grace told me it is a very abstract concept and I shouldn't feel too badly if I haven't been able to grasp it yet.

Monique and Charles left this afternoon. He tipped my face up and stared at me as if he was trying to remember every zit. Then he kissed me on the top of my head again and I felt about two. For a second I wished I was two and that he could pick me up and carry me around. It was so regressive and stupid. At least Monique didn't try to hug me again. I made sure of that.

Mavis and I stayed up last night to watch TV and see the giant ball drop at Times Square. I wouldn't be caught dead in a crowd like that, but I searched the faces when the camera zoomed in during the countdown. I can't help searching faces in crowds, even though I probably wouldn't know my mother if I actually saw her.

While I was home I watched a nature show on TV where they were raising baby condors in captivity, using puppet mother condors to feed and stroke them so they wouldn't bond with humans. But when they released them into the wild, there was no mother condor to show them what to do.

I go back to Our Lady's on Tuesday. I wonder if there's snow there. Everything here is so bare and cold with nothing to cover it.

Your person,
Taswell

Tuesday, January 5

Dear Mavis,

I wish you hadn't left before I did. It was lonely in the apartment without you for three days. It makes me realize, though, that you're right. It's better that I live away at school than be by myself so much. You're wrong about Grace being an authority figure, though. She doesn't tell me what to do but does help some of us with spiritual guidance.

Would you please order some new uniform skirts for me in the next larger size. Must have been all the great food over the holidays.

All the girls think the jacket is awesome.

Your loving granddaughter,

Taswell

Tuesday, January 5

Dear Pim,

I just wrote to Mavis and tried to make her think I have friends other than Grace without actually saying so. It seems so important to her.

Would you believe, there was a letter waiting here from Charles when I got back. I still haven't opened it. I'm not sure why.

Grace's brother, Simon, drove her back here, and I saw him just as he was coming up the steps with some of her things. I didn't know she had a brother and certainly not one so drop-dead gorgeous.

"He's much too old for you," she said right after he left. I guess she couldn't help noticing how I stared at him. "Anyway," she said, "he's entering the seminary next fall."

It must be a family kind of thing, like some vocation

pocket or something. I wonder if her younger sister will escape it.

It made me think, though. You know, he hasn't entered the seminary, yet. And his being older and everything would be just perfect, like St. Joseph—someone to take care of the baby and me at the beginning and to look out for me as Charles does for Monique, that is, if I wanted someone like that and if it wasn't, you know, physical. Though maybe a baby prophet really only needs a strong single mother. I'll have to meditate on this one. It would sure help if you could give me some other signs. I'm so in the dark here.

Everybody brought back so much stuff—new stereos, cameras, computers, clothes they'll probably never wear. It's disgusting. Madeline's father gave her a new car, even though she can't even drive yet. Can you believe it? She was dangling the car keys in our faces all through dinner and the other girls got gushy and silly about it *ad nauseam*.

Grace wanted to know why I brought back the Christmas ornament. I told her it had special meaning.

Your person,
Taswell

Dear Taswell,

I think the visit was very successful, don't you? I was a little worried at first. But the chip on your shoulder has definitely slipped some, and nobody got hurt. Amazing! You and Monique seemed to hit it off, too. She's such an open, loving person that I knew you couldn't resist her.

And you—you are growing up so fast. I want to freeze you at this lovely adolescent stage. I want you to stay wide-eyed forever, like some baby owl, your long dark hair brushed back from your spectacled face. Of course, I know you're growing up and will soon be a beautiful young woman with a life of your own. I hope, as you grow, that you'll begin to understand me better and to realize that I have always loved you. Always.

Next Christmas we want you to come to Paris. There are so many things to show you. We need to make up for all the lost time, the lost years.

Love,

Father

Dear Pim,

Now, just because I restrained myself and didn't do something antisocial, my father thinks Monique and I are great pals. It isn't going to be *that* easy, Charles. Sure,

I can tolerate her. But don't expect some cozy family thing. I'll have to get this across to him, Pim, somehow. And all that "we" stuff at the end of the letter. It's too late now to be him and me. And it's too late now for anything like what he wants.

Sister Edwina has us reading William Blake. I'm beginning to love it, especially the poem that goes "Tiger, tiger, burning bright/in the forests of the night." Did you know Blake was a visionary? He could see his angel and other ones besides. He even drew their pictures. If I was a visionary once, like when I was four, why aren't I one still? Why don't you appear anymore? Just once. What do you think of "Blake" for a name? It doesn't look that great when I write it down. I think I know what the name will be, anyway. I think you do, too.

Your person,
Taswell

Saturday, January 9

Dear Taswell,

Yes, I'm glad you realize that keeping you home with me would not have been the solution right now. It was great fun having you for the holidays, and I'm sorry, too, that I had to leave for the Coast. Beatrice has been moping around ever since you left.

I thought having Charles and Monique worked out well, too. Isn't she a perfect delight? I suspect you were sorry about that subscription to *Playgirl* once you'd met her. But, goodness! How gracious she was! I was most impressed.

I'm glad to see that you're putting on some weight, but do hope you won't overdo it. It seems too soon to be replacing uniforms purchased only last fall. Perhaps you're having a growth spurt. Your mother shot up in the ninth grade as I recall. I'm also sending the vitamin supplements you asked me to get, though it doesn't look to me as if you really need them.

At any rate, it was a great comfort to see you in the flesh, so to speak, and to realize that my decision to send you to Our Lady's was a good one. Of course, being too thin is never good, but you don't want to get too chunky either. Cut out the sweets, and your problem will be solved.

Fondly,
Mavis

Wednesday, January 13

Dear Pim,

So now Mavis thinks I have a weight problem. No one here seems to have noticed anything. Not even Grace, who has really got that detachment thing down pat. I just wish she didn't detach from me so much. Since we've been back, she seems to need all this time alone. She still teaches my religion class sometimes, and we talk after class. And she did tell me before that the imposition of silence was going to be an important part of her novitiate. I just didn't expect it to be imposed so soon. She is becoming a lot like Edna.

The more I try to detach from the girls at my table for meals, the less annoying they become. I've actually entered into their conversation, if you can call it that, a few times. When I mentioned Mavis, I was surprised to learn that Madeline's father is the head of a rival publishing house. Madeline probably doesn't work too hard in school because she can always get a job as a secretary there and be as silly as she wants, or she can live off her inheritance. She obviously has no plans to contribute anything to the world.

Apparently, all the other girls exchanged meaningless gifts at Christmas. I'm just glad I didn't know about it. I can't relate to any of the things they get so emotional about.

"I saw Blue Man Group over break and was just blown away," squeals Madeline. I wonder if she was able to stay quiet long enough to actually hear them.

I had accepted the fact that girls my age never talk about anything of substance. But then Stacey brought up Grace's brother, Simon. Seems everyone had seen him besides me.

I don't think I was revealing anything when I told them how he's entering the seminary next year. I didn't want them to keep their hopes up. It felt strange to have them all pester me for details, though. It must be a little how it feels to be popular.

Have to do my Latin now. Even if it is a dead language, I've decided that under the circumstances I should be able to at least read it. Maybe you know it already, and we can converse. Maybe I'll compose a prayer in Latin. I'm pretty good at conjugation, too.

amo   *amamos*

amas   *amais*

amat   *amant*

Sort of sing it, and it sounds like a lullaby.

Your person,

Taswell

Thursday, January 14

Dear Charles,

It was very nice seeing you and Monique at Christmas. Thank you both for the money.

Monique looks very healthy for someone expecting a baby. I am sure you will both be very happy.

Your daughter,

Taswell

Dear Pim:

I wrote to Charles last night. Of course I had to thank him, but I'm not going to say anything to support his dream that he and Monique and her baby and I are suddenly a family. And I'm not going to gush over Monique like he wants. The way he loves her, she doesn't need anyone else. I figure I'll just be very polite, in keeping with my present state.

Madeline and Stacey came to my room last night. It was as though they wanted to hang out or something. I didn't know what to do with them because I only have one chair and it was full of stuff, but they sat right down on the floor. Stacey didn't say much, but, of course, Madeline never stops. She had questions about everything—my pictures, my new jacket, the book on birthing customs.

"If you want to know anything about that, about the gory details," she said, "just ask me. My sister just delivered twins at home, and I was there for it all."

"Delivered" made it sound as if her sister did it by herself. It would be ironic if Madeline really could answer some of my questions. Maybe it's another case of what Sister Winifred says, of God working in strange ways. Imagine Madeline, Madeline the goofball, being Madeline the messenger!

"Maybe later," I told her, trying not to sound too interested for now.

"Where'd you get the Christmas ornament?" she asked. She even picked it up and turned it over to see the "made in Thailand" on the back.

"It was a gift," I said.

"From who?"

"From my guardian angel," I said. They both laughed, and it seemed to shut her up.

I wasn't surprised when she maneuvered the conversation around to Simon. I had to pretend to know more about him than I do. Maybe when Grace has time to talk to me again, she'll tell me what I need to know. Just in case they ask again.

I weighed myself after gym and have gained six pounds.

Anything more you can tell me? This waiting around is the pits.

Your person,

Taswell

Friday, January 8

Dear Taswell,

I seem to remember you saying something, or Mavis saying that you keep a journal. I admire you for doing that. I have never been able to keep one even though I think it's such an important way to understand yourself and other people. I do like to write letters, though, and thought we might start a pen pal thing. I had one once—a pen pal in Canada while I was in school in France. Unfortunately, we lost track of each other.

I'm sorry you and I didn't get to be better friends over the holidays. Perhaps I wanted it too much. Maybe we can start fresh and you will see that I'm not trying to take your father from you. Quite the contrary. You are both very much alike, you know, so earnest and intense and yet unsure. Perhaps that's why you have such a hard time connecting with each other.

I expect you're very busy at school after vacation. But when you have the time, I hope you'll write to me. For starters, I need to know what Mavis might like for her apartment. Charles and I would like to send her something special to thank her for her hospitality. I thought you would know better than anyone else.

Love,
Monique

Friday, January 15

Dear Pim,

Pen pals! How infantile! Did you know about this, that Monique was thinking up something so . . . so banal? And the way she says Charles and I are alike. Intense, maybe. But unsure? I'm as sure as can be about things, about the important things. I'm probably the only fourteen-year-old girl in the whole world who knows what's in her future for absolute certain.

And what can Monique and I possibly write to each other about? If it wasn't for that question that needs a definite answer, I would just ignore her letter.

Well, I am busy, and she can wait.

Your person,

Taswell

Tuesday, January 12

Dear Taswell,

This will have to be short and sweet. Wilfred is sending me to the book fair in Nice. It's a very small book fair, so I hadn't expected to be going. Actually, he is going, too. It will be nice to have a traveling companion. Luckily you and I had those few weeks together, so you will not feel that I am deserting you.

Beatrice will have my itinerary if you need to reach me. Unfortunately, I didn't have a chance yet to order the uniforms. I'm sure it can wait another two weeks.

Delighted that you are making friends at last.

Fondly,

Mavis

Saturday, January 16

Dear Pim,

Who is Wilfred? Can it be her boss, Mr. Binder? She's always called him Mr. Binder. Mr. Binder this. Mr. Binder that. Wilfred? If it's really Mr. Binder, he used to have a wife. But that's right. She died. Mavis went to the funeral last summer.

She's wrong about the uniform skirts. I already keep the placket open and use giant safety pins to hold the skirt together. In two weeks I won't be able to breathe. And what is all this time she thinks we had together? Yes, Mavis, I feel deserted. I feel deserted a lot.

The strangest thing happened in social studies. We were talking about jobs, about what we want to be some day. I said a great philanthropist. Everyone laughed, naturally, because they hadn't a clue what the word meant. But then Madeline said she wanted to be a midwife. Can you believe it! Now if that isn't a clear message! She talked all about her sister's midwife and how calm and strong she was, qualities it's hard to associate with Madeline. But, even though it's pretty incredible, she's obviously the one, *the one* I must eventually share my secret with. *When* is the question. It musn't be too soon. Will it be possible to swear her to secrecy? Will you look into some special kind of grace for that?

Your person,
Taswell

SEVEN

Dear Taswell,

I thought you'd like this card. It not only shows the hotel where I am staying (which is quite luxurious in an old European way) but the magnificent harbor. Perhaps I can take you here some day. In fact we might plan a long trip on the Continent for next summer. At the end, you could stay a few weeks with Charles and Monique and get to know your half sibling.

Quite a nice little book fair! Quite an enchanting few days!

Fondly,
Mavis

Dear Pim,

I got a postcard from Mavis. She's in love again. I know the signs, the breezy little "Isn't life wonderful" exclamations, the exciting plans for my future. Well, the timing is probably good. She'll forget about my "weight problem" for a while and my so-called social life. She'll forget everything but books and what's-his-name.

I am making a concerted effort to befriend Madeline. She seems a little confused by this and surprised when I actually acknowledge some of her inane comments. The girls at our table appear relieved that they can talk about other things while I listen and exclaim, listen and exclaim. It is somewhat isolating in a very agitated way. How will I ever get her to listen to me?

Your person,
Taswell

Dear Monique,

Mavis likes old things—old clocks, old prints, old men. Whatever. I'm sure you'll think of something.

I don't know why you think I keep a journal or who could have told you that. I do write letters, as you point out, but am already very busy writing to certain specific people.

Maybe it's just the idea of having a pen pal that you miss.

Sincerely,

Taswell

Dear Taswell,

Well, it wasn't much of a letter, but you did write and I am very glad of that. I suppose I deserved that last remark. You are good with words. A very clever girl all around. You would think such a person would not have any difficulty at all figuring out when someone is genuinely fond of her. I have no hidden agenda, Taswell. I'm not offering you anything but friendship. And that, it seems, is fraught with all kinds of monstrous possibilities.

Perhaps sometime you will actually need me, and I will be here for you. Remember this.

Love,

Monique

Saturday, January 30

Dear Mavis,

You must be back from your trip by now. I hope you and Wilfred had a very nice time. Isn't he the one with the dead wife? Have you ordered the uniform skirts yet? I really, really need them.

I have become good friends with Madeline Lemieux. You may know her father. He is President of Odysseus Publishing, Inc. You will be happy to know that I no longer stay in chapel for most of the lunch hour. I know you worry about things like that.

Did you tell Monique that I keep a journal? I write letters, Mavis. It's not anything like keeping a journal. I did write in my diary when I was very very young. Perhaps that's what you remember.

I am going to help Madeline with her math during evening study hour, so will have to go now. She says she has been diagnosed with math phobia, but I think she is just having trouble with the basic concept of listening.

Remember the skirts. Please!!! I could also use a big sweater.

Your loving granddaughter,
Taswell

Saturday, January 30

Dear Pim,

It is impossible to help Madeline with math! She is like paralyzed on the left side of her brain. But it doesn't seem to bother her at all, so why should I worry. We worked maybe half an hour on her homework. That is, I worked on her homework and she looked out the window or chattered. When I couldn't take it anymore, we went for coffee in the Commons. Actually, I had

Sprite instead, because I've read coffee isn't good for unborn babies. Makes them jumpy or something. This baby jumps without coffee. Sometimes I think it must be gas, but other times it's piercing, like a foot kicking.

Madeline asked about boyfriends. I guess she has a few and has actually dated since she was twelve or so. I felt really sexually retarded admitting that I don't know anyone of the opposite sex very well. I did tell her Mavis won't let me date until I'm sixteen, which makes it more understandable. How will I ever be able to make her understand about the other stuff? How am I going to lead up to it or get her to believe me?

Maybe you are planning something to convince her. If you aren't, maybe you should be. More signs. Some really divine intervention. Could you please get to work on it?

Your person,
Taswell

Monday, January 25

Dear Taswell,

We received an invitation to Parents' Weekend in May. I'm going to do all I can to arrange my schedule around it. But I wanted to check it out with you. Monique thinks I should go alone. Is that what you'd like? She thinks you and I should have some time together. Just tell me. We'll do whatever you like.

We visited briefly with Wilfred Binder and Mavis in Monaco. They make a very attractive couple. She's been a widow for so many years. I would like to think she's found happiness at last.

I saw a group of schoolgirls from some local convent taking the Metro—to the Louvre, perhaps? They were with a sister in a blue habit with a pleated white wimple, and the scene looked like something straight out of *Madeline*. (Do you remember how I used to read that book to you and how you loved it?) How I wished you were with them and that you would be coming home to my apartment for pizza or whatever it is American girls like best. There is even a McDonald's here, so you would feel right at home.

It is hard to be a father by long distance. It was beyond me when you were small, but I hope you'll let me make up for that.

Love,
Father

Sunday, January 31

Dear Pim,

Charles wrote to ask if I want him to come to Parents' Weekend by himself. That's exactly what I want. Why would I want her here? (If Mavis comes, she'd better not try to bring Wilfred Binder.)

And Simon came to see Grace again. He hung out

in the Commons with her for a long time, but I just couldn't bring myself to go up and talk to them. Other kids did. They'll know now that I was bluffing about having so much information about him. He is truly gorgeous—light chestnut hair like Grace's, eyes like a postcard sky, Mentadent teeth. He'd be so perfect. As a caretaker. You know.

I did get a chance to ask Madeline some stuff. She just loves to talk about her sister's labor, so it wasn't hard to get her going on that. I found out a lot about contractions and she demonstrated this really weird breathing. When she talked about the head crowning and fetal monitoring, she kind of lost me, but she sounded so medical that I was really impressed.

Still—how am I ever going to tell her about me?

Your person,

Taswell

Monday, February 1

Dear Grace,

I am writing you this note because it is so hard to find a time when you can talk with me. I wish you didn't have to be so silent all the time. I really liked it when we had real conversations.

What I want to ask about, what I am sure you'd know, has to do with Parents' Weekend. Charles, my father, says he will come alone if I want him to. Without Monique. I should be glad about that. Right? But she tries to act so nice sometimes that I get confused. I don't want to betray my own mother.

Please answer this when you have time. I don't know who else to ask.

Your friend,

Taswell

P.S. I saw Simon talking to you for such a long time. Has he changed his mind about being a priest?

Monday, February 1

Dear Taswell,

I'm sorry that you take my silence as something personal. I think I should explain to you that I'm not here as a counselor but as someone trying to learn how to be a nun. Mother Viano has had to remind me more than once that this pursuit should be taking all my attention.

Sometimes, Taswell, I think you see big problems where there aren't any at all. Perhaps it has something to do with your very active imagination. Why are you so dead set against liking Monique? Why are you resisting what seems to me to be a very healthy fondness for her? How can you betray a mother you've never known?

And, no, Simon hasn't changed his mind. I can't imagine what all you girls see in him! He can really be a pain sometimes.

Your friend in Christ,

Grace

73

Dear Pim,

If you would just communicate more openly, I wouldn't have to ask Grace for advice.

She really wasn't much help this time. Maybe she's becoming too pious or something. And complaisant. That's the word I'm looking for. "Exhibiting a desire or willingness to please; cheerfully obliging." And she wants me to be as complaisant as she is. Well, I'm not planning to be a nun. My vocation is for something more active and worldly. But I have to be really careful about my attachments. And my detachments, too. Come to think of it, that's probably at the root of all this confusion. I've lost sight of the practice of detachment. It sure won't be hard to detach from Wilfred.

Your person,

Taswell

EIGHT

Dear Pim,

I've found out one thing. If you don't answer letters, you don't get any back. For now, that's just fine with me. I'm trying to be very focused and centered, to concentrate on the little prophet that is growing inside me. I shut my eyes and concentrate on sending her all my strength and all the love my mother would have given to me.

Mavis finally ordered the skirts and they just came. Not one minute too soon! I've gained ten pounds. I was shocked when Madeline commented on my "moon face" and said that I should stop eating in between meals or I'll be as fat as Sister Bruno.

It is hard to be centered around Madeline, who has

begun to think we are best friends. Since I have never had one, she could be right, though I doubt it. It has been necessary to spend a great deal of time with her so I can work up to my revelation. We have talked about her sister's labor so much I want to puke. We've discussed all Madeline's "dates" since the age of ten and all the times she almost but not quite went all the way.

For my part, I have been sort of laying the groundwork by telling her about the other virgin births I've read about besides Mary's. One article said some of these might be explained by the remote possibility of one egg being fertilized by another, and, if this happened, the "resulting embryo" would always be female. Unfortunately, Madeline is not very interested, and I find it more and more difficult to insert this kind of information into our so-called conversations. Only yesterday she said, "I don't know why you're so hung up on this virgin birth thing. It's like so unnatural."

I just laughed. I mean, she's got to be more receptive before I tell her the truth. Right?

Your person,
Taswell

Tuesday, February 2
Dear Charles,

I think you should come to Parents' Weekend by yourself. I think it would be better that way. Monique will be very pregnant by then. My friend, Madeline, says she probably shouldn't travel.

I'm glad you remember how you used to read to me. I thought I was the only one who did. I pronounce my friend Madeline's name to rhyme with "fine," like the book title, but no one else does, not even her.

I wish I could remember my mother. I wish you could remember her face. Monique is probably glad that you don't.

It is late and I'm very tired.

Your daughter,

Taswell

Wednesday, February 3

Dear Pim,

Sister Bruno actually stopped me in the food line tonight and told me to take smaller portions. That sure is like the pot calling the kettle black. She pinched my cheeks together with one beefy hand and said I am suffering from Freshman disease and she is going to cure me. If she only knew how hungry I still am even after dinner, how I can smell her sauerbraten or meatloaf or stew all the way down the hall and how it makes me salivate like some ravenous dog. The coconut cream pie has an odor I can't begin to describe. It's like perfume. Madeline says Sister Bruno is right and she will help me control my appetite. They are like in cahoots now. If it wasn't so painful it might be funny.

It made me think, though. If even Sister Bruno, who hardly ever leaves the kitchen, is noticing something, maybe it's time to tell Madeline the truth. Sometimes I forget why I decided she had to know in the first place. She'll never understand in a million years.

Can't you do something?

Your person,

Taswell

Tuesday, February 2

Dear Taswell,

It hardly feels as if Spring will soon be upon us. I always forget how windy March can be and am disappointed when it doesn't warm up right away. Where you are, so close to Canada, it still must feel like winter. As a girl, I loved Spring skiing in Vermont and was upset to learn that you had skipped the recent school trip to Stowe.

Charles and Monique sent me a beautiful etching by Dürer. They said you helped them with their decision. I had no idea you had such exquisite taste. Charles has always had impeccable manners, whatever his faults. Wilfred thinks it strange that I treat him like a son-in-law when he did, in fact, rob me of my daughter. But that was such a complicated relationship, and your mother made mistakes, too, and unfortunate choices. The choices you make when young can affect your entire life and the lives of others. I hope you will always remember that and think carefully about every decision.

Here I am sounding like the voice of doom when I am really quite light-hearted and optimistic. Wilfred seems to have that effect on me. He thinks that you should begin calling me "Granmere." Would you like that?

Fondly,

Mavis

Dear Mavis,

Wilfred's suggestion is silly and weird. At my age I'm not going to start calling you something completely different. Why is it every time you fall in love you get so out of whack? I thought you were through with that kind of thing. I thought when people got old they became more dignified.

I should have told you before that, just in case you're serious about it, I won't be able to take a trip with you next summer. There is something else I'll need to do. And I don't know a thing about Dürer. I just told Charles and Monique you liked old things. Sorry to disappoint you.

Your loving granddaughter,

Taswell

Dear Taswell,

If that's what you want—for me to come alone—that's what I'll do. Your friend Madeline is probably right about it being a bad time for Monique to travel. I'm glad you have such a sensible and good friend. The friends you make at this time in your life, you sometimes keep for years. I still have a friend from the fourth grade. Pete Cooper. I think you've met him. When we see each other, it's like fourth grade all over again.

Monique is swimming at our club right now. The doctor says swimming laps is very good for her and the baby. If she were here, I'm sure she'd send her love.

Love,

Dad

P.S. Monique has made me realize that "Father" is so formal, and "Charles" so impersonal.

Friday, February 12

Dear Pim,

What is all this name changing! Do they really care *what* I think? And all that stuff about keeping friends for years. It makes me tired when I think of Madeline's voice going on and on and on forever.

Of course *I* don't belong to a club and there is no indoor pool here for me and *my* baby. Even if there were, wearing a swimsuit would be a dead giveaway. Monique doesn't have to worry about any of that. She doesn't have to worry about anything, and is probably in the greatest shape of any pregnant woman on earth. Well, I can't expect the perks. I knew that from the beginning.

Thought you'd like to know I did try planting a few more hints with Madeline in study hall. We had no monitor at all and were able to talk. As long as we keep it down, nobody usually checks.

In Health class we're supposed to be learning something about "procreation." We actually don't learn much, but at least it gave me a chance to bring up the subject again with Madeline. I asked her what she'd do if she ever got pregnant by accident, and she said she never would because she'd be so careful. I said, just for the sake of argument, what about an accident or what about those girls who claim they've never done, you know, anything, but get pregnant anyway? She said she didn't believe those girls and she wasn't going to worry about accidents, especially not now with no boys within a three-hundred-mile radius. I asked her where she got that statistic and she said, "Don't you know anything? There's a school for boys in Windmere, the next town over. It's called St. Basil's. Everybody knows that. Where have you been?"

"Well, just for the sake of argument," I said again,

"what if I said I was pregnant when I don't even have a boyfriend and have never been, you know, like sexually active. What would you say then?"

"I'd say you must by lying," she said. "I'd say you must have gotten pregnant in the summer or over Christmas break or by running down the mountain in the middle of the night all the way to St. Basil's."

"Now that's just ridiculous!" I told her.

"And so is you being pregnant," she said.

"What about," I said, "Divine Intervention?"

"Divine Intervention!" she wailed. "You are really crazy! That kind of thing only happened in the Bible. It doesn't happen anymore. And it certainly wouldn't happen to you or me or to anyone else in this anemic pseudo-monastery."

The last part didn't sound like her. She admitted that her sister is the one who calls it that, when she isn't referring to it as "The Convent of the Curiously Inept."

You've got to help me with this, Pim. You've got to!
Your person,
Taswell

Wednesday, February 10

Dear Taswell,

Such a short little note! I seem to have touched a nerve asking you to refer to me as some form of grandmother. When you were born, of course, I felt far too young for such a title. But years and situations change things. Perhaps I should not have mentioned it in a letter, however.

Wilfred, himself, is a grandfather many times over and feels quite comfortable being called Granpere. It was his suggestion, you see. But we can discuss it another time since you seem so opposed.

I have had a very surprising letter from Sister Eduard. She asks if you have ever had an eating disorder or were subject to great weight fluctuations in the past. You did look a little chubby over the holidays, but I thought we had addressed that and that you were doing something about it. Once one puts the weight on, it isn't easy to take it off. She does mention that you seem to have made a good friend. I am very relieved to hear it from her. I'm well aware that sometimes you tell me what you think I want to hear.

I have a manuscript to read before tomorrow, so will have to say good night now. I will send Louise Collard's book, *Making Friends with Food*. You remember her. She prepared that wonderful mushroom, leek, and cranberry stew for us the last time she was in New York.

Fondly,
Mavis

Dear Mavis,

There seem to be a lot of messages in your last letter that it wouldn't take a genius to figure out. 1. You and Granpere = a pair. 2. Your "situation" has changed and may not include me. 3. I am a liar.

The first two I obviously can't do anything about. The last is not exactly true. By the way, I hated that stew.

Your loving granddaughter,

Taswell

Dear Pim,

I think Mavis is tired of having the responsibility for raising me. I must be really slow not to have seen through all this glittery family stuff lately with Monique and Charles. I guess Mavis is a lot like my mother in other ways besides hair and eyes and stuff. She wants to run away from me, too, but have a nice safe place to put me.

I'm really tired. I can't write any more tonight. I don't think I'll write to anyone for a while, not even to you.

Sometimes, so I can go to sleep, I imagine God's hands. They're giant size, big enough to climb into when they meet together like a cup. I think they're the only place where I truly fit.

Your person,

Taswell

Dear Pim,

Thank you, thank you, Pim! You did it! You came through for me!

Madeline knocked on my door really early this morning, even before lauds. As you must know, I've begun saying the appointed prayers for the seven Canonical Hours every day, which means I have to get lauds over with before morning mass. It was still dark, with me and Madeline probably the only ones awake except for Edna and the nuns. Madeline was still in her nightgown, her yellow hair all wild like a lion's ruff, and her face white as flour. She pushed me back into the room and closed the door as though there was something coming after her.

"Taswell," she said in a hoarse whisper, "I've had the strangest dream. It was like, so real. Like a movie only so bright I woke up with a headache." (The headache thing is getting to be a dead giveaway. Maybe you should think of something else next time.)

Then she said that I was in the dream, standing on a globe with the moon and stars under my feet—just like the statue of Mary at the end of the hall on our floor. I was moaning and calling her name and she was arranging all these strange primitive medical instruments on the big picnic table outside the dining hall. She said she was really calm and everything but that I wouldn't get off the darn globe and lie down so she could get busy and deliver my baby.

After saying the word *baby* she stopped and looked at me as if she'd never seen me before. "Why," she asked, "why would I dream a dream like that?" Then she paused and sort of scowled, her forehead as pleated as a lampshade. "It's all that stupid talk about virgin births. You're so obsessed with the subject that the whole stupid thing has gotten into my dreams."

"What if," I said, really slowly in case she was going to go ballistic, "what if I told you that your dream is trying to tell you something?"

"Yeah, like maybe you're really pregnant," she said. "Or that maybe you're really a bird. When I tried to pull you down you turned into that repulsive Halloween hawk."

It was too early in the morning for this. I didn't know where to begin or what to say next. "Let's stick with the first part, with the baby and why you might dream something like that?"

She, like, tore at her hair. "I told you," she said, "because you talk about it all the time. You stuffed so much of that kind of thing into my brain, that it's spilling over into my dreams."

"Oh, very scientific," I said, "for someone who wants to be a midwife."

Then she said, "And that's probably part of it, me

wanting to be a midwife and you always talking about virgin births. It got me confused."

"Then why are you so upset?" I asked. It made me cold to look at her. She was standing in the middle of my narrow room, her bare feet on the bare floor, not even hugging herself to keep warm. I jumped back into bed and pulled the quilt around me.

"I told you," she said. "Like it was so real and because of the colors and the really bright light."

"Maybe because it *was* real. Maybe because it was a real visitation, some higher being imparting information. Think of how the angel told St. Joseph in a dream that he had to take his little family into Egypt," I said.

"And like you're so holy and I'm St. Joseph!" she snapped at me, really pissed this time. "Sometimes I wish I never gave you that Christmas ornament. That I'd never wanted to be your friend in the first place."

"You gave that to me?" I couldn't believe it.

"Well, I thought you should get something from someone," she said. "All the rest of us were exchanging gifts."

"I don't believe you!" I said.

"Believe it or not," she said. "It's no skin off my back. I just thought you needed a friend."

"I do," I said. I said it reluctantly. It made me angry that anyone, any one of those girls, would think that. "But not for the reasons you think."

She started acting really suspicious and stepped back toward the door.

"What other reasons could there possibly be?"

It seemed like forever before I could get the words right and actually come out with them. If you were trying to inspire me, then, Pim, it wasn't working.

"Good reasons. Sacred reasons," I finally said. "I need someone, I need you to deliver my baby." I pulled my nightgown over my belly so it rounded out. "I need you to help me deliver her."

"Your baby! Her?" she shouted at me.

"Yes, *her*," I said. "Remember how Father Cleanth said the world needs a prophet for the New Millennium and how it might be a woman. Well, he was absolutely right." I grinned at her. It was so wonderful to be able to finally tell someone. "And I need you to help me deliver her."

Your person,

Taswell

NINE

Wednesday, February 17

Dear Pim,

It is Ash Wednesday. Lent is just beginning and I should already be planning some sacrifice, something in addition to saying the Canonical Hours, which isn't easy seven times a day no matter what. Sister Bruno has suggested I give up sweets. I don't think I can do that.

It looks as if I will have to give up being friends with Madeline if she doesn't start talking to me soon. Ever since I told her my secret yesterday morning, she's been acting strange. She avoided me all day, and at dinner she hardly spoke to anyone. The other girls must have noticed, because when she's so withdrawn, she's like another person. I still don't know if she believes me or what, and it will be impossible to find out if she keeps avoiding me. Everyone thinks we've had a fight.

Second Installment.

As I was writing this, Madeline opened my door and walked right in, slumping down in the middle of the clothes pile on my chair and looking like a sleepwalker, as if she didn't know where she was or why.

"Hi," I said, and she managed to say it back. Then neither of us spoke for a long time until she began to talk to the floor. At least that was how it looked. She never once looked at me. This is how it went.

"I didn't believe you."

"I didn't think you did."

"You have to admit, it's pretty fantastic."

"I thought you'd feel that way."

"And I feel like you've been using me."

"I need to use you. You're part of the plan."

Then she did an amazing thing. She sort of sighed and said, "Yes, I guess I am."

It was incredible. It was like this absolute perfect statement of belief.

"I've thought about this all day yesterday and today," she said, "and it all seems to add up. The way you've been so distant from the rest of us; the way you're getting really thick through the middle like my sister did, your enormous appetite like hers, and how you say you stopped having your period months ago. I do think you must be pregnant. And I don't think you could have ever slept with anyone. It's just not possible."

I didn't like her saying that last part, implying that I'm some incredible geek. But it doesn't matter. It only matters that she believes me.

"But will you help me?" I had to know.

"I guess I have to," she said. "I mean that dream and everything. I guess I'm expected to. It's pretty scary, though. Nobody's ever expected me to do anything important before. I sort of exaggerated about the help I gave my sister. I mean, I was there and everything, but I didn't really *do* anything."

She looked as if she was going to cry.

I suppose I could have told her about you, then, Pim, but I think it would have been more than she could take. At first I was disappointed about the ornament, but then I thought how maybe you inspired Madeline to give it to me and that it really was a kind of sign.

I told her not to worry about the whole thing too much. To trust in God and all that stuff. But I hadn't anticipated how nervous she'd be. I mean, when Madeline's quiet, there's something terribly wrong. And the things I was saying didn't seem to be helping. She was back to that stricken look she'd come in with.

Suddenly, she shot up, and almost ran through the door, saying, "Gotta go now. I still have French homework."

How are we going to discuss this calmly if she's going to act like a jerk about it? How are we going to make plans? Well, there's still lots of time. I figure the baby won't be born until the end of May or the beginning of June. Easter would have been nice—the Resurrection and everything. But at least now my baby will have a day that's all her own.

Your person,
Taswell

Friday, February 19

Dear Taswell,

Well, now I understand just how rude some of your letters can be. I had thought your father was exaggerating.

You cannot expect all our lives to revolve around yours, my dear. Nor are we trying to influence you in some sinister way as you imply. You will always be more than a granddaughter to me. Another daughter, really. But whether or not my life moves ahead should have no bearing on what direction yours will take. You are often as willful as your mother and as self-absorbed. When you decide to leave me, too, who will fill the emptiness in my life if not someone like Wilfred, who adores me?

I will not demand an apology for I believe you wrote that last letter in the heat of the moment. I do hope you will consider all I've said.

Fondly,
Mavis

Dear Taswell,

We have been trying to think of names, and wanted your input. Though Monique had an ultrasound, we told the technician not to tell us the sex of the baby so it would come as a complete surprise.

Neither of us likes "junior" added to names. What do you think about Jean Luc or Noah for a boy? We both like Anabelle or Danielle for a girl. Of course, there's no hurry. We just thought you might have a favorite name that we haven't considered.

It's been raining for days, and, of course, the rain cuts down on our walks around the city. You'd like where we live, so close to many major attractions and my office, but with a very pretty enclosed garden. Still, we've been thinking it would be nice to have a country house and we've done some looking on weekends. I wish you could look with us, and I tell Monique that we must find someplace where we can easily grow raspberries. Once, when you were a very little girl, you ate so many you got hives. Do you remember?

Well, Easter is almost here. I'll be seeing you very soon after that.

Love,

Dad

Dear Pim,

Can you believe that Mavis actually said that Wilfred "adores" her? The dictionary defines adore as "To worship as God" or "To regard with deep, often rapturous love." I think it's sacrilegious!

Well, I do believe Charles probably adores Monique. But isn't Mavis too old to be adored? I told you she gets silly when she's in love. I can't imagine anyone ever adoring me. Anyway, it would be too weird.

Madeline has lost her appetite. She just kind of stirs her food around or doesn't show up for meals at all. I hope she snaps out of it before any of the nuns notice. Stacey says she is worried about her. Maybe I should be, too, but I think she's just still in shock. I will give her *Making Friends with Food* when it comes.

I, myself, am feeling much better about everything. A few of the nuns have been making remarks about my posture and weight, but I'm certain they haven't guessed the real reason. Right now I'm glad to be big boned like Charles.

I'll have to put this down and go to vespers in Chapel even though I prefer to say them by myself. Everyone is required to attend during Lent. The few sick and dying nuns have rooms with windows over the altar. They open right into the mural of angels and saints. Grace calls them anterooms for heaven. Sometimes you can see a curtain blowing back or a hand on the sill.

I will pray hard for Madeline. I'm sorry she feels so burdened by all of this. I thought she would be excited like me. I thought it would give her a purpose in life.

Your person,

Taswell

Thursday, February 25

Dear Taswell,

I am writing you this note in the infirmary. Sister Brigid says she'll get one of the other girls or Grace to take it to you. I don't think I'm really sick. But I do feel awful—very shaky and funny. Sister Brigid asked if I've had bad news from home. Don't worry. I didn't tell her what's really the matter.

But I've just got to tell you that I've changed my mind. Not about believing you, but about being able to help. What do I really know about delivering a baby? What I remember most is all the blood. There was an awful lot of that. And what if something went really wrong? What then? You've got to find somebody else for this. I know you pray a lot, so you've got to ask God or whatever saint you're in touch with to let me off the hook. Please do it soon. Let me know when you've found a replacement.

Your friend,

Madeline

Dear Madeline,

Weren't you afraid Grace would read the note you sent? I don't think she did, but you should be more careful after this.

I'm sorry if you don't want to take on this responsibility because I clearly think you're going to have to. You're the one that was chosen. There's no one else.

Maybe you're coming down with something. Everything looks bad when you're tired or sick. I'll bet you'll feel differently after a good night's sleep.

We'll talk about it tomorrow. And remember. Be careful what you put down on paper.

Your friend,

Taswell

Friday, February 26

Dear Pim,

Why in the world did you or your associates pick Madeline! Unless you drown her in grace, she'll simply fall apart. I know I shouldn't doubt the ways of the Lord, but it's hard holding on to hope where Madeline is concerned.

I am going to go visit her in the infirmary in a few minutes, and I plan to be extremely firm. She can't back out now. I won't let her!

Your person,

Taswell

Dear Charles,

I'm too old to start calling my caregivers by completely new names. I hope you understand.

As for names for children—what about Aileen for a girl? If it's a boy, you can call it Charles. If it's boy and girl twins you can call them Aileen and Charles. If it's girl twins you can call them Aileen and Taswell.

It is nice that you're going to buy a country house. It will be a good place to raise lots and lots of children. You will probably need to think of lots and lots of names.

Your daughter,
Taswell

Dear Pim,

I visited Madeline in the infirmary yesterday, but when I tried to be firm with her, she became all weepy and gross. Sister Brigid told me I was upsetting her patient and made me leave. Now Madeline will probably become sicker and stay in there forever. I thought telling someone else would make everything much easier. But it isn't working out that way at all.

And you're not being any help either, Pim. Imagine how much harder it would have been for Mary if the Angel Gabriel had been as invisible as you are! Oh well, I guess you can't help it that you're not part of the Seraphim. Are there any steps or tests to take for advancement? Maybe the way you manage this entire scene is one of them? If it is, I don't think you're going to get the golden wings or whatever.

Your person,

Taswell

Saturday, February 27

Dear Mavis,

I have been thinking about it, and I guess you're right that I don't always tell you the truth. I'll try to do better. Sister Edwina says that if people are going to believe us about the big things, we have to gain their trust in the little things. I may have something big to tell you about very soon, and I want you to believe me when I do.

Since we don't get a Spring break, I won't be able to come home for Easter Week, but there's going to be an Easter brunch here and we can invite our families. There isn't too much chance of snow then, so even if you don't want to drive all the way with Emil, you could take a plane from the airport in Montpelier. Please, please come, Mavis. I miss you so much.

Your loving granddaughter,

Taswell

Dear Taswell,

No, we do not plan to name the baby Aileen after your mother. Of course you knew that wouldn't be a welcome suggestion. I thought you'd want to be included in a family decision, but obviously I was wrong. As for lots and lots of children, one child is what we're looking forward to right now.

Sometimes I think you and I are having a meeting of the minds, and then you pull a letter like that out of what—years of resentment! Or are you just trying to be a little too clever? I was never around teenaged girls much, not even when I was a teenaged boy. It would help if you'd try to meet me halfway. Resentment is an ugly cloud that colors everything.

Monique sends her love.

Love,

Dad

Wednesday, March 10

Dear Pim,

Sister Eduard called me into her office today—during gym. I'm having more and more trouble with that medicine ball and sometimes sit out and pretend to have cramps, so I thought she wanted to see me about that.

Unfortunately she wanted to talk about my "eating disorder" and my "continued antagonism" toward

Madeline. I guess there have been more letters back and forth between Sister and Mavis.

When I tried to tell her that Madeline and I are friends now, she said she has ample proof from Sister Brigid that this is not the case. Sister Brigid has told her that I've been bullying Madeline and that she's afraid of me.

Well, it's true that Madeline has continued to avoid me. I tried to tell Sister Eduard how Madeline and I have been hanging out together and everything, but she acts as if I've just been setting Madeline up for something because of some deep-seated antagonism and because I think she's stupid and easily led. I did think that, but I don't anymore. Actually, I kind of admire Madeline for sticking up for herself. I've even begun to like her, and I like sharing this secret. I can't imagine why she's afraid of me.

So now it turns out that I have to start seeing Sister Francesca, the school psychologist, two mornings a week right when I should be saying tierce and having study hall.

I know exactly what it's going to be like—all the delving for what's really at the bottom of things. If I actually tell Sister Francesca anything real, she'll think it's a symptom of something else. They always think that. And, of course, I can't tell her the truth. Not yet. I just have to find a way to talk to Madeline before Sister Francesca does.

Your person,
Taswell

TEN

Dear Pim,

I had to skip vespers in Chapel so I could hide in Madeline's closet and talk with her in private when she came back to her room. Even though I couldn't see to read the prayers in the dark, I know them pretty much from memory. It is really very peaceful in a dark closet by yourself. I just wish this one didn't have such an overpowering Madeline smell.

As I crouched there it began to seem like a bad plan all of a sudden. I mean, it was bound to frighten her if I jumped out and be even worse if she discovered me there. I was about to leave and devise some other way to confront her, when I heard the door from the hall open and steps into the room. Madeline talks to herself, so I knew right away it was her. Most of what she goes on about is in the form of orders like "Don't forget your notebook, bird brain" or "History, pages 365 to 400. Before tomorrow. Do it!"

But this time she let out a giant sigh, and I could hear the bed squeak as she threw herself on top of it. Then I heard, "What a relief! She wasn't in Chapel. Maybe she'll start leaving me alone."

How insulting! I hadn't done anything but look at her (firmly) since she'd been let out of what Sister Brigid, the ex-marine, insists on calling "Sick Bay."

It was getting really hot in the closet, and I was beginning to feel a little sick myself, when she opened the door and threw her sweater at me. I figured the pile of clothes I was sitting on had arrived there in the same way, so she obviously hadn't seen me and wouldn't if I didn't make any noise. I'd just have to wait until she left and then make my escape. When I heard her shampoo bottles knocking together, I figured she was on her way to the showers. And when the door opened and then shut, I jumped out.

I was standing in the middle of the room when Madeline rushed back in, saying, "You always forget something, nitwit," to herself. She gave a scrunched up kind of scream when she saw me, like someone had stuffed a sock in her mouth. It was her own knuckles.

"Don't be afraid," I said right away, aware that I was

sounding for all the world like some visiting angel myself. "Please, don't be afraid of me."

She was white as a mime, and I wanted to reach over and pinch her cheeks to make her look alive. And she was speechless. Bad sign!

"I just want to talk to you. I was waiting in your closet, but then I thought how that might frighten you, so I was trying to leave before you got back."

She started backing away like I was an apparition, the hair on her head actually seeming to bristle.

"Just calm down. Will you calm down? What are you afraid of? Why have you been avoiding me?"

She started to cry.

"What else can I do?" she said. "How else can I keep you from forcing me to help you with your . . . your . . . mission?"

I had never thought of it in those exact words, and it was a very good way to put it, so I told her so.

"You can't flatter me into doing what you want," she said then. "I've made up my mind. Sister Francesca says I must not allow you to manipulate me any longer."

"You're seeing Sister Francesca, too? It figures." Then I had an awful thought. "And I suppose you've told her everything."

"No," she said. "I wouldn't do that. They'd probably throw you out of school. And they wouldn't believe you the way I do."

"You still believe me?" I asked. I had to smile.

"I can't help it. I wish I didn't," she said.

I tried to explain then how if she believed me, she had to know that she was chosen, too. She had to see that she was part of the mission. She had to accept it the way that I did.

"I can't," she said, crying harder and making little frantic snorts. "Don't ask me about it anymore. You act like I have to do what you say. But Sister Francesca says we always have choices."

"It isn't what *I* say," I told her on my way out. She wouldn't look at me. "It's what God says."

Your person,

Taswell

Dear Taswell,

I just felt like writing to you today. You don't have to write back. I was wishing that I could talk to my mother and tell her about my baby. Sometimes I do talk to her, but, of course, she can't answer me. And I often talk to the baby. It made me think how your mother probably talked to you, too, before you were born. How she must have loved you, sight unseen, loved all your little movements within her, loved taking you with her wherever she went, loved the bloom on her own face when she looked in the mirror, coming directly from the child, warm and safe inside her. I'm sure she wanted to keep you warm and safe forever. When she found that she couldn't, she must have used all that enormous love in making the terrible decision to leave you behind. Wherever she is, she must have missed you every day of her life. I know I would.

Love,
Monique

Tuesday, March 16

Dear Pim,

Monique's letter came right before my session with Sister Francesca. Why would she write me a letter like that? For some crazy reason I started to cry and couldn't stop, like when I was little and would get all gulpy and breathless. When I came into Sister Francesca's office, I was sure my eyes were red, so I kept my head down and was determined not to break down in front of my interrogator.

Sister Francesca is the "good listener" kind. She sits there and waits until I have something to say. If I don't say anything, she just keeps sitting there. Then she ushers me out when the time's up.

I guess she's gotten tired of waiting for me to speak, because today she started asking questions, ones like who are my friends and do I make friends easily.

Without really looking at her, I told her the truth.

I said I have two friends—Grace and Madeline. She did her "Hmmmm" thing. I said how I didn't usually make friends at all, but that I thought I needed friends right now.

"For your purposes," she said, which really startled me.

I figured she was just fishing, though, so I said, "No, because it's kind of lonely here, and I thought it was time to branch out."

"Branch out?" she asked.

"You know," I said. "Learn how to socialize. With Madeline, I'm trying to do that. With Grace—I've thought about it, and she's a sort of mentor, I guess. She knows a whole lot more than most of my peers."

"So you are looking for a role model," she said.

"Sort of," I said.

"Well, that's a very mature endeavor," she said. "And Grace and all your teachers say they find you a very bright young woman. Why, then, do you suppose, you act in such an immature fashion with someone your own age, with Madeline?"

I told her I wasn't sure what she meant. It's not a lie. I'm not sure.

"I'll put it another way," she said. "Why do you choose to bully her?"

"I don't," I said.

"Madeline says that you do," she shot back at me.

A light went off in my head.

"Look," I said, "if I stay away from Madeline, if I promise to leave her alone, can I stop coming for these sessions?"

She made a tent out of her fingers and held them in front of her face, her elbows propped on the arms of her chair as she tipped it back. She stayed that way for ages.

"There are deeper issues here," she said finally, "far deeper, I suggest, than even you are aware."

The buzzer on her little egg timer rang then, and it was time to go. Not a minute too soon!

Tonight I talked to my baby for a long time. I told her how I'm going to love her forever, how she will never have to try to explain herself to somebody like Sister Francesca because there is one person who will know all about her from the very beginning and it will be me.

Your person,
Taswell

Thursday, March 18

Dear Mavis,

You must have been in on it, so I'm sure you know that they're sending me to a counselor now—a nun who actually looks more like a banker—very serious and jowly. And she wears a suit all the time instead of a habit, because she also works at the mental hospital near here. It would probably not be a big deal at all to get me transferred over there. My care could continue undisturbed.

These boring sessions are really a waste of my time and Charles's money. Just thought you should know that. I'm doing exceptionally well in all my classes except gym. Some of the greatest thinkers of our time have been socially maladjusted. Were you aware of that? On the basis of the many biographies I have read, it's usually the geeks who grow up to do something really important. Maybe if you straighten me out too much, I'll be totally useless to society. I suggest you give this some thought. An individual's brain should be sacrosanct ("regarded as sacred or inviolate") and not tampered with unless it becomes totally unwired. At least that's my view.

By the way, the rumors that I am bullying Madeline are untrue.

You haven't answered about coming for Easter brunch. Sister Bruno says she has to have a head count soon. Please come. You could go to mass with me before. It's an awesome holy day, the most important one in the whole liturgical year.

Your loving granddaughter,
Taswell

Thursday, March 18

Dear Monique,

I got your letter. I never thought about my mother knowing me before I was born. If I had a baby, I could never leave it, so I don't really understand that part.

Taswell

Thursday, March 18

Dear Pim,

Another boring session with Sister Francesca. She sat staring at her fingers, and I sat staring at the floor most of the hour. You could hear the chimes on the clock in the corridor as if it were in the room with us. She, herself, has a very noisy way of breathing—probably still has her adenoids, like Stacey—and she clears her throat a lot. I was counting the seconds in between throat clearings to see if the intervals were the same, when she suddenly said, "Perhaps we should discuss your plans for the future. What do you think you'd like to be someday?"

I wanted to be consistent so I said, "A philanthropist," like I had in social studies. Only *she* knew what it meant and sort of smiled.

"That would imply someone who has a great deal of money to give away," she said. "Are you someone in that category?"

"No," I said, "but it might also mean someone who

has other things to give away, like themselves."

"An interesting way of looking at it," she said. "But that doesn't exactly answer my question. Presumably, unless you are independently wealthy, you will need to do something to make the money that you plan to distribute, or—sticking to your definition—to develop the talents or qualities that might prove useful to others."

"I have thought about being a dancer," I said then, to throw her completely off the track. (Sister Kathleen will be sure to inform her that I am delusional.) "Or a nun." (They love it when you say that.)

"Well, now," she said (see!), "then you do plan to give of yourself. That's encouraging. Can you provide some example of the needs you hope to meet? For instance, what might your target population be? Whom would you hope to reach?"

"The world," I said. It slipped out before I had a chance to think about it.

"The whole world?" she asked in dead earnest. Her little eyes got beady and dark.

"Why not?" I said then, and laughed so she'd think it had all been a joke.

She breathed a sigh of what—relief? Exasperation?

The egg timer buzzed. She jumped. I couldn't get out of there fast enough.

I hope you are working on an alternate plan, Pim, or

have some idea how to get Madeline to change her mind. For my part, I'm still working on trust. Oops! Time for compline.

Your person,
Taswell

Dear Taswell,

What a shame that you can't come here for Easter. Unfortunately, I won't be able to go to you either. Wilfred's grown children always celebrate together on that day, and they are anxious to meet me. Since your school will not be closing down and none of the other girls will be leaving, you'll not be alone. The thought comforts me. How often I wish it were possible to be in two places at once.

Wilfred and I, however, will be coming to Parents' Weekend. With Charles there, as well (though I understand you instructed him not to bring Monique), it will be a little reunion.

You will like Wilfred. Everyone does.

While I think of it, I wish you wouldn't hint at mysterious future events in an effort to inflate your own feelings of self-importance. You have always been subject to such flights of fancy, as when you told your second grade class that we kept a tiger in the basement of the apartment complex and had a swimming pool on a boat that you neglected to describe as a two-man turn-about. I had hoped you had given up that sort of thing.

Fondly,
Mavis

Dear Pim,

I'm beginning to think Sister Francesca dreads these meetings as much as I do. She seems so totally bored, which is good. I try very hard to keep it that way. Maybe she'll tell Mavis and Sister Eduard that I'm not interesting enough to be insane. If she only knew how interesting I really am! How one day I and my child will be in history books or in the New New Testament or something.

Today she wanted to know about my compulsive "observance of rituals." I don't like her referring to my prayer life like that, like some illness. Why does the Church instruct you to say things like the Canonical Hours and the Angelus at certain times if they're going to then tell you it's compulsive? I asked her that, and she didn't have a good answer. Just something about how saying one's "Office" is usually reserved for the clergy.

Then she changed her question and asked why I pray so often.

"Does this have something to do with your vocation?" she asked.

"What vocation?" I said, forgetting.

"To be a nun," she said, with a sneer. "I had an inkling you weren't serious about it."

"I just said it was a possibility," I said. Anything's a possibility.

So I tried to think of something else possible in order to answer her question and came up with being a visionary like William Blake and writing canticles of praise.

"Very ambitious," she said. "You aim high. Next time bring me some of these...uh...canticles."

Oh no! How does she see through me like that?

"I didn't say I *had* written them," I said, weaseling, "I said I wanted to write them."

Then she wanted to know if Madeline and I had ever talked about our "aspirations," and I said yes, and did she know that Madeline wants to be a midwife.

She said she believed Madeline had thought of that at one time but had changed her mind.

"Why?" I asked. "Why would she do that? She wants to be a midwife. I know she does."

Sister Francesca wanted to know then why it was so important to me what Madeline had in mind, and I suddenly realized I'd dropped my guard and was acting upset about something that shouldn't be any of my business.

"Because she really is my friend," I said, "no matter what any of you think. And she was so certain before. It was like her 'Calling.'"

"I see," she said. Just like that. "I see."

What does she see? How much does she see? What if Madeline has let something slip? It's pretty easy to do around this lady.

When the buzzer went off, she didn't move from her "I see" position with her face under her finger tent. I wondered if she was falling asleep. But then she sort of came back to life and looked hard at me.

"Taswell," she said. "Is there anything you want to tell me?"

"No," I said.

"A burden is sometimes lifted by sharing it with others." She stood up and patted my shoulder with her stiff little hands.

Had this trick worked with Madeline? I had to know! But how could I find out?

Any ideas, Pim? This is crucial!

Your person,

Taswell

ELEVEN

Dear Mavis,

The weekend was really dull. All the weekends are that way except when Grace takes us somewhere in the school van. She took everybody to see some weird puppet maker on another mountain yesterday, but I stayed here and worked on my history paper. With everyone gone, I didn't have to wait for one of the computers.

I wish you were coming for Easter and not going someplace with that Wilfred person. I'm not really surprised, just disappointed. I wish you weren't bringing him with you for Parents' Weekend. He's not my parent. He's not even related to me.

Making Friends with Food just came. I'm loaning it

115

to my friend who has lost her appetite.

I will not be in the play or the Irish Step Dancing presentation for Parents' Weekend, but I'm the only tenor in the choir since Stacey's emergency tonsillectomy, and I think you will be proud of some of my projects. My ant farm is multicultural—red and black ants living together, or almost. Side by side.

Your loving granddaughter,

Taswell

Dear Pim,

It is Holy Thursday, and we are all going to be in the procession tonight. It is a solemn procession, and we're going to be wearing our white cheesecloth veils from Retreat Week. Everything will be in Latin, which is so cool. I would advise you not to miss it.

I plan to get in line in back of Madeline somehow. When we're just waiting around, maybe I can make contact with her. Of course we are supposed to be silent, so I'll have to be careful. Any diversionary tactics you can devise would be greatly appreciated, like a small incense fire. Just a suggestion.

Have to go now.

Your person,

Taswell

Thursday, April 1

Dear Pim,

Don't let two letters in one day go to your head. I just thought you deserved to be kept up to date.

First, we were arranged by height for the Procession into the Chapel, so I couldn't stand next to Madeline. When we finally sat down in the front row pews, however, I found that I was directly behind her—clearly your doing. But I wonder if you realize how impossible it is to whisper to someone sitting in front of you. I did manage to kneel once while she was still seated and say something quickly into her left ear. She twitched and almost fell onto the kneeler.

All I said was, "There is no possible replacement. It's got to be you."

Through the rest of the service she seemed to be trying to hide under her veil and didn't look back at me once. Even going up for communion she kept her head down and wouldn't look up. When I happened to look down myself and saw my own ankles I was shocked. They look just like Sister Kathleen's. All the other girls seem to be growing sleeker and more like women while I am growing swollen and square. I hate all these body changes, but I guess it can't be helped. I must concentrate on the glorious outcome.

There was hot chocolate and doughnuts in the cafeteria afterward. I would have taken mine to my room because lately I feel like people are watching me eat, especially Sister Bruno. But I stuck around tonight to try to talk to Grace and to Madeline if at all possible.

Grace asked me if I'd like to help her with the Easter Egg hunt. Sounds like something you'd do in kindergarten, but I don't want her to tell Sister Francesca I'm uncooperative, so I agreed to blow and decorate eggs with her on Saturday. How do you blow an egg? I used to dye them with Beatrice years ago when I was a child.

When I asked Grace about her brother she said something about how that's all anybody asks her about now. So I inquired about her dogs and then asked, "How is your silence?"

"It isn't *my* silence," she said. "It's not something you can own. The 'imposition of silence' is a condition. It's like there's this big sign saying 'QUIET PLEASE' and I have to observe it. Understand?"

Of course I knew that. I just didn't know how to ask about it.

"And how is your detachment?" she asked.

In all the business with Madeline, I had totally forgotten about it. I honestly don't know what to do with it at the moment.

"I've been working on the virtue of trust," I said.

"It's really the virtue of Faith," she said. "Trust is just a manifestation of faith."

"Right," I agreed. She's going to be such a great nun. I mean, who would know that!

"What's all this trust for?" she wanted to know. "What are you worried about?"

"You're beginning to sound like Sister Francesca," I said.

Then she told me how she'd heard I'd been meeting with her and asked if it was helping me.

"Help would imply that I have a problem. Which I don't," I said. "I go because I'm told to go. The virtue of obedience. Right?"

"Right," she said, looking very strange, like she wanted to cross her eyes but couldn't. Why was she looking like that?

I never did get near Madeline. There were bunches of people around her all evening. But there was a note under my door when I got back to my room.

"Even if you don't find a replacement, it can't be me. If I learn how in time, I'll drive you to the hospital. That is, if there isn't anyone else. But that's it."

What hospital. I can't go to a hospital!

I'm getting scared, Pim. I'm feeling fat and clumsy and scared. I wear my sweater all the time, now, even when I'm too hot. Have to find bigger safety pins somewhere or some elastic.

Your person,
Taswell

Dear Pim,

Good Friday would have been the pits if it hadn't snapped me into realizing that my suffering is nothing compared to Christ's. The Mass of the Presanctified was so solemn, and that awful hollow sound of a stick against wood instead of bells ringing stayed in my head all day long. When we hold lighted candles in the darkened church tonight for Holy Saturday, I'll be holding mine for my baby and me and renewing my baptismal vows in preparation for her birth and baptism. It's almost too beautiful to bear!

Blowing all those eggs this afternoon made me tired and breathless. Grace asked if I felt okay. I wanted in the worst way to tell her the truth. Why didn't you choose her to help me instead of Madeline? How about changing your mind? Please think about it. Madeline seems to be a lost cause.

Your person,
Taswell

Sunday, April 4

Dear Mavis,

I'm glad you called, but I wish you wouldn't put Wilfred on the phone after this. It's no way to introduce someone. We had absolutely nothing to say to each other.

Thank you for the scarf. I'm glad it's so big. You're right that I don't need candy right now. Charles and Monique sent me some chocolate truffles. I will give some to Grace and allow myself one every four days.

We had an Easter egg hunt, but I chose not to participate. You'll be happy to know that I did help to prepare the eggs. If you have never blown an egg, you should. You make a pin prick on both ends, and blow on one and out shoots all the goop inside. Perhaps Wilfred would like to try it. (See, I am not ignoring him and pretending that he doesn't exist, the way you say.)

There were lots of parents and aunts and uncles and other extended family members here for brunch. I wonder if you could say I have an extended family. I guess it is more an extended nonfamily. Anyway, they stayed until late in the afternoon. Even Grace's family came and five of Edna's six brothers, who are as loud and noisy as she is quiet. Grace's brother, Simon, is still going to be a priest.

I missed you, Mavis.

Your loving granddaughter,

Taswell

Saturday, April 3

Dear Taswell,

Only a few weeks until Parents' Weekend. I really am looking forward to seeing the school and meeting your teachers and friends. Since you say you're happy there, I've tried to revise my objections to the place. I'll feel better having seen it for myself, though.

Monique is feeling pretty uncomfortable and having a hard time sleeping. We've been walking all over this city at all hours. Wish you could come along, especially now the weather is so mild.

I'm sending you something that I've kept for a long time. Your mother left it in my car one night many years ago.

It should be yours.

Love,

Dad

Saturday, April 10

Dear Pim,

Charles sent me a handkerchief embroidered with the letter A. It is all white—cloth and embroidery—and washed and pressed and smells like carnations. He must have kept it in a special place.

It's not like inheriting a parent's ring or anything. But it's so awesome knowing that it's something my mother touched and carried with her. I'll keep it forever or someday give it to my daughter.

I'm not having trouble sleeping like Monique. I like die right after lights out. It's as if I can't get to sleep fast enough, as if I'm sleeping for two. I should probably begin walking more, though. Up and down the halls is the best I can do here. If I start doing it while I pray, it will take care of two obligations and everyone will just think it is that odd Taswell doing some new odd thing, but I can't worry about what people think. The only thing that matters now is the health of my baby.

I wonder if Charles will notice anything about me when he comes. I've begun wearing my blouses outside my skirts and am waiting for the first demerits for uniform infraction. With my sweater on, though, no one seems to notice, and it's still cold enough to wear one all the time. The heating is abysmal, as in "Very bad" rather than "Very profound. Limitless." There are a number of abysmal necessities around here, such as showers that never get hot. It must be great not to have to worry about things like that.

Someone is knocking on my door. Be right back.

Second Installment.

It was Grace. What a surprise! And she wanted to come in and talk. But it wasn't the hanging around kind of talking like I'd hoped. It was as if she'd been commissioned. Like she was some emissary ("An agent sent on a mission to advance the interests of another.") But who sent her? At first I thought it might have been you, but she wasn't telling and she didn't actually get down to her true reason for being here, until she'd hemmed around for about five minutes. It was so uncool for Grace. I was mildly disappointed.

She didn't want to sit down right away either, pacing

back and forth, the way she does when she's teaching Religion.

Finally, she wove her long fingers together and flexed them as if she were thinking deep thoughts. Then she shoved my laundry onto the floor, plopped down in the chair, and said, "I've been worried about you, Taswell. About your... appearance."

"I would think appearance would be the last thing to concern an almost-nun," I said. "I would say you may be getting off track."

"Listen to me, Taswell. Hear me out. This is no time for your flippant remarks." She looked almost desperate, so I kept still. I can do that, you know.

"I've noticed, many of us have noticed, that you're gaining an unusual amount of weight."

"Lots of girls gain weight," I said.

"But not so much in one place," she said. "Before you came here to school or when you were home on break... was there any... did you"—and then she stopped and actually threw up her hands. "It's so preposterous. I can't imagine that I'm saying these things to you. You're such a child. Hardly even a teenager."

"I'm not such a child," I sputtered. "I'm probably the most responsible girl in this school. Responsible enough to be singled out."

I stopped myself.

"Singled out," she repeated. "What does that mean?

What can that possibly mean? What are you telling me?"

"It doesn't mean anything. I'm not telling you any-thing," I said.

She started acting very distant then, getting up and backing away, just as Madeline had. Was she going to be like her in other ways, too? Was she going to start being afraid of me?

"We'll talk about this later," she said super slowly, as though I must be retarded. "We'll have a good long talk when I have more time and you've thought about what I've said."

"What's to think about?" I said. "You didn't say any-thing except that you thought I was fat. Lots of people get fat."

"But not all of a sudden, Taswell." Then, "But I said we'd discuss it later."

And she was gone.

Your person,

Taswell

TWELVE

Monday, April 12

Dear Pim,

I don't know how to even begin to write about this. I don't know whether to be angry at you or what. Is it okay to be angry at a celestial being? But where in the world were you? Why didn't you let me know, or give me some support or something? I have never felt so completely alone in my life!

You had to have known about it—the way, when I opened the door for my hour with Sister Francesca, they were all going to be sitting there like a jury, arranged in a semicircle of chairs facing the door. When I arrived, this feeble little smile sprang from one mouth to the next as if it were connected by rubber bands. The whole row became one giant smirking Cheshire cat—

Sister Francesca, Grace, Sister Eduard, Sister Edwina, Sister Eugenie, and Sister Bruno.

But my amazement faded as soon as Sister Francesca started to speak. She wasn't going to wait for me this time for sure.

"Taswell," she said with icy calm. She is always calm. "Please sit down, dear."

The only other chair was facing the group, so I sat in it and pulled my sweater around me, feeling terribly cold.

"This is not an interrogation," she said then.

"What is it?" I asked.

She couldn't speak for a moment. She obviously hadn't thought of a name for it. But then she said in this pleased-with-herself voice, "It's a friendly discussion."

"Then why don't I sit with the rest of you?" I asked.

This didn't please her. She stopped smiling.

"No," she said. "I think this arrangement will do nicely."

There were murmurs of agreement.

"We have a number of questions to ask you."

"To interrogate," I muttered. "'To examine by questioning formally or officially.'"

"As you will," Sister Francesca said, with a sigh. "But we are not interested in playing word games or any other kind of games with you, Taswell, as you will soon discover."

Sister Francesca was, I guess, just at the beginning of her turn, which was obviously first. I couldn't believe it as the words flowed from her like little rivers. (She must have been incredibly stopped up in all our earlier sessions.) For a while, in fact, I thought she wasn't going to give anyone else a chance. She gestured and squirmed while she spouted all kinds of stuff about my attitude, my appetite, my appearance.

"The three a's," I thought, trying to stay interested. Sister Eduard really got my attention, though, when she interrupted with the words "religious fanatic."

"Religious fanatic!" I exclaimed. "Religious fanatic!"

"Please, Sister," Grace interrupted. "I think you're being a bit harsh. I would hardly call Taswell a religious fanatic. Though she does seem too attached to a number of compulsive rituals, her desire for spiritual development is quite sincere."

"A sincere fanatic, Sister Eduard." Sister Francesca seemed to be joking, but she caught herself with a quick laugh. "You do realize this kind of fervor is not uncommon in girls of her age. There is cause for concern, however, when someone begins to carry such things to extremes."

"I am more concerned with her appetite," interrupted Sister Bruno.

"And her appalling attitude," said Sister Eduard.

They battled together awhile until someone, maybe

Grace, got in the word "appearance" again, and I felt all their eyes upon me at once. You could hear a small communal gasp after they asked me to stand. Like a bunch of ladies' maids, they gently removed my sweater, tucked in my blouse, fussed over the safety pins, and examined the profile of my body.

"She does look somewhat pregnant," said Sister Eugenie at last.

"Impossible," said Grace.

"Well, it might explain all the rest," said Sister Francesca.

My silence seemed to make them even more agitated. But it wasn't the time or the place for my revelation. It was too soon. And they were not in the least receptive. You obviously hadn't prepared any of them, Pim, in any way. They were clearly thinking only of physical aspects, and it would have been impossible at that moment to make them aware of my mission, of my great blessing. Apparently, Madeline has not revealed my secret either. They are completely concerned with outward signs.

When I wouldn't tell them anything, Sister Francesca said that Doctor Philips would be called in to examine me again. They're just like Saint Thomas, needing incontrovertible ("unquestionable") evidence. Well, some of it they're just going to have to take on faith. Which is where you come in, Pim. You've got to be ready to zap them as you did Madeline. You've got to do it somehow, someway!

Your person,

Taswell

Dear Taswell,

Another sleepless night. Sometimes the baby seems to be pressing all the way into my throat. Charles is away on business or we'd be off walking, even if it is one in the morning. Since I don't relish walking alone at night, I thought I'd swaddle myself in this big overstuffed chair and write to you.

Night and shadows make me reflective. I can't help wondering what this child will be like. I hope he or she will be smart like you. And funny. You have a very original sense of humor, even if it is sometimes at the expense of others.

It makes me think that when you grow up, you'll be very compassionate. You see all sides—the dark and the light, the funny and the solemn. It is a good—even a great—quality.

I've found myself thinking of you so much this afternoon and evening that it feels a little like you're reaching out to me. I have never been anything like clairvoyant, so it's hard to believe I'm dreaming this up. In fact, I have this incredibly strong feeling that I should be there with you right now. But, of course, that's impossible. When you get this letter, you'll probably laugh at how silly I'm sounding. It must be another one of those expectant mother moods.

I'm glad you'll have a chance to spend time alone with your father soon. He's looking forward to it so much.

Love,
Monique

Friday, April 16

Dear Taswell,

What do I do? They keep asking me questions. I don't know what to say. This is so awful!!

Your classmate,
Madeline

Saturday, April 17

Dear Pim,

You'd think they were sticking pins in her or something. Why can't Madeline just keep quiet, like me?

And when did she suddenly get to be my classmate instead of my friend?

If you count the difference in time zones, Monique was thinking about me at almost the exact same time I was being questioned by "the committee." It's pretty spooky. I do need someone's help, but it's going to have to be divine.

She sure does seem to like me. I don't get it.
Your person,
Taswell

Saturday, April 17

Dear Taswell,

I'm taking a chance in writing this to you. They want me to have no further contact with you until you begin to tell us what's going on.

But I have to warn you that you stand a good chance of being expelled. And something about this whole thing seems so strange—completely out of sync with anything I know about you. Even though you badly want somone to love, I can't imagine your ever having had an opportunity to get pregnant. Forgive me, Taswell, but you are just plain ignorant when it comes to normal human relations. Unless, of course, it's a Virgin birth!

I'm sure the truth is completely innocent. Just tell everyone, and things will turn out all right.

Your friend in Christ,
Grace

Sunday, April 18

Dear Pim,

It's so incredible. Somehow you did it. You informed Grace, and now there are three of us who believe. If you could do that so easily, I'll bet it won't be long before the others accept my message too. It doesn't have to be all of them, Pim. I don't have to have absolutely everyone on my side.

Thank you, Pim. Gratia. Gratia. Gratia.

Everything is going to be all right.

Your person,

Taswell

Dear Pim,

You probably know already that Madeline was waiting for me in Sister Francesca's room when Grace came to get me today—looking tired out and jumpy, like some cornered animal. Madeline stares at me now as if I'm from another planet, and Sister actually patted her arm when I came into the room and said, "There, there. I'm here with you, dear. Taswell can't threaten you here."

It's no fun being treated like some creature from the deep, especially when you haven't really done anything. It was Halloween all over again, and I'd thought we were way past that.

"We want to talk facts this time," said Sister Francesca, and she told me to sit on the other side of her, which was as far away from Madeline as possible, who, when I passed her, actually shivered. It made me feel bad.

"We want to know the truth this time."

133

Then she turned to Madeline. "Don't be afraid to tell us what you know. Though you have mistakenly tried to shield Taswell in the past, you can help her today by simply telling the truth."

She kept harping on the truth. The truth. Until Madeline was getting popeyed. I was prepared for her to burst out with something at any moment. But instead, she made loud whiny denials, swearing she didn't know what Sister was talking about.

Finally, Sister Francesca turned to me and said, "You have sufficiently frightened this poor child. I can't imagine why she's being so loyal to you under the circumstances. What are you holding over her head?"

I told her it was okay with me if Madeline told her anything she wanted to. Actually, I was beginning to think that it might be better if it came from Madeline, but I could see she wasn't up to it.

It was then that I was inspired. (Finally!) It came to me all of a sudden, but without the bright lights or anything, and no headache (thank goodness), that this was the time, *the* time to tell all—before Dr. Philips examined me and presented her version of things and I was made to feel like an outcast. But where to begin? Maybe if Grace were here, too, and there were two believers on my side. So they sent for her in the room next door, and when she came into our room she had this uncomfortable little smile that made her look kind of annoyed.

"Taswell wanted you here," said Sister Francesca. "For moral support, I suppose. I was about to ask her who the father is?"

Grace drew in a quick breath. Madeline's eyes got large and wet.

"Well, it's obvious that she's pregnant," Sister said. "There's no point in beating around the bush any longer."

She was helping me more than she could possibly know by getting right down to the nitty-gritty.

But then there was this awful silence like a sudden dark sky. When I realized the next person to speak had to be me, I started to sweat actual cold dribbles. I tried to think quickly while choosing my words very carefully. Not easy.

"Grace and Madeline are my witnesses to the truth," I began.

But Grace interrupted with "What are you talking about? Why are you dragging me into this?"

"I'm about to tell Sister Francesca what she's been wanting to know. That's all. I've been entrusted with a great responsibility and I need those persons present who have been divinely inspired to believe in me."

Madeline nodded her head up and down like a robot. Her eyes settled back in her head. But Grace's eyes were wide and flashing.

"You're talking nonsense, Taswell," she said. She turned to Sister Francesca. "Really, sister, she's not crazy.

She just has this incredibly active imagination."

"I have not imagined *this*," I said, sticking out my belly. "And I have not imagined being singled out."

"She has been," said Madeline.

"In what way?" asked Sister Francesca, somewhat breathless.

"Why, singled out as the person to have this baby. To bear a child who will be a prophet for the New Millennium. And her name shall be called Aileen, which means "Bearer of the light.""

"Oh dear God," exclaimed Grace. "When I said that about a Virgin birth, Taswell, I was only kidding."

"*She's* not kidding," said Madeline, smiling now and looking almost relaxed, in a fidgety way. She stood up, as if she might bow. "It came to me in a dream."

Sister Francesca's mouth opened and shut like a blowfish.

She gave a wordless, throaty moan before slipping under her finger-tent again. For a while it looked as if she was never going to come out.

Your person,
Taswell

THIRTEEN

Monday, April 19

Dear Taswell,

I haven't told a soul about your...condition and about how you broke the news to Sister Francesca and everything. I swear it. But some of the kids were asking me all kinds of leading questions after volleyball practice, especially when you didn't show up. It's obvious they know something. I just wanted to make sure you know I'm not the one who told them.

Do you think it could have been Grace? Would she do that? You know her better than I do, but it seems to me she'd be the last person on earth to spread rumors.

Where were you all afternoon?

Your friend,

Madeline

Dear Madeline,

I knew you'd be at dinner, so I'm just going to slip this note under your door.

I told Sister Eduard that I wasn't feeling very well, and she said it would be all right to skip afternoon classes and for Sister Bruno to bring me supper on a tray. Sister Eduard said she wasn't feeling very well either. I wonder why? And it was pretty weird how Sister Bruno rapped on the door just now and left the tray outside. When I picked it up, she was halfway down the hall, like there were wild dogs at her heels.

If it was Grace who told about my revelation, you couldn't exactly call it spreading rumors. I mean, it's true. It's all true. Maybe she was, like, inspired to tell. Maybe that's *her* mission, to spread the news. I hope it is, because up until now it was as if she were being sort of left out, and I felt bad about that.

I guess I'll have to expect people to stare at first. I wonder if they'll treat me differently? Of course, they always have, but maybe now it will be out of interest instead of indifference. You'd better be prepared for them to stare at you, too, the way you have such an important role to play.

I suppose we should just try to act normal, whatever that is. After all, it will be some time before anything actually happens. Everyone will probably be used to the idea by then. I would appreciate your thoughts on all of this as I am feeling sort of nervous. It's like somebody's expecting me to make a speech or something.

Your friend,

Taswell

Monday, April 19

Dear Taswell,

I don't think anybody is expecting you to do anything. And none of the girls at dinner seemed to be too clear on what's going on, so I doubt if Grace or someone told them any of the details. If you don't come to classes tomorrow, though, they might get suspicious. I think that part about acting normal is good. But you have a lot of leeway there. No one ever seems to know what you're going to do next.

Actually, I have always admired that about you, Taswell. Have I ever told you? Probably not.

Your friend,

Madeline

Monday, April 19

Dear Pim,

This has been the strangest and longest day. In some ways I feel relieved that my secret is out, at least to a few people. Still, it was really nice when it belonged only to me, and I could keep reminding myself of that fact.

Of course, you always knew. I don't know what I would have done if you hadn't been in on it from the beginning.

Right now, I feel as if I could sleep for two or three days. It's like I've been in this giant marathon or as if I've been running without stopping for weeks. Tomorrow I'm going to have to act as if nothing's changed even though everyone else either suspects something or knows about it.

Perhaps the nuns will try to make an example of me. Do you think they would do that? I'd better read a few chapters about the North American Martyrs, so I'll know how to conduct myself, just in case.

Your person,
Taswell

Tuesday, April 20

Dear Pim,

People—the girls and the teachers—have been very quiet all day. Very quiet. It's as if they're all carrying the library around, the way snails carry their houses on their backs. No one has been talking much in class or passing notes or anything. I don't get it. When Sister Edwina called on me to recite in English, she said, "Remain seated, my dear. No need to stand," as if I'd come into the room on crutches.

Is this what Limbo is like? You know, the place where

the babies go who haven't been baptized. I've always thought it was supposed to be a pretty nice place, even if a little boring. But the dictionary calls it "A region or condition of oblivion or neglect."

I didn't want a fuss to be made over me exactly, but I wasn't prepared for oblivion or neglect just yet. And Madeline manages to be surrounded by people or duties whenever I want to talk to her. "I have to run to the office for Sister Bruno." "Sister Eugenie needs me to make copies before next period." She's never been so busy or in demand in her entire life!

One of the upper classmen, somebody named Theresa, stopped me in the hall. She just stood there with her hands on her hips and glared at me as if I were a worm.

Then she said, "You're not fooling anyone, you know. I hope you're proud of yourself!"

"I am," I said.

"Oh," she spouted. "What gall! What unmitigated gall!" And she stomped off to join a little group of whisperers.

I'll have to look up *unmitigated*. What a great word!

I'm beginning to hope that Stacey or someone, anyone, will come right out and ask me to tell them exactly what's been going on. I mean, I can't announce my important news to people who don't seem to want to listen. And, of course, I haven't been examined yet by Dr. Philips, so I can't really *prove* anything. She's coming to the convent tomorrow, though, and after she gives me all her tests and presents Sister Eduard with the incontrovertible (unquestionable — remember?) evidence to the absolute truth of all that I've said, I'm telling everyone! I'm telling the world!

Your person,

Taswell

FOURTEEN

Wednesday, April 21

Dear Pim,

When she said it, when she said, "You're not pregnant, Taswell," I felt as if the words were coming from someplace at the bottom of the mountain, that they weren't real words and it wasn't a human voice saying them. I'd been looking out at the trees and suddenly the window panes were dark and flat with no images coming through. My eyes were forced back into the room to the tight face of Dr. Philips, her thin lips delivering words into the air as if they were little balloons that had no power and were doomed to pop. But all at once, they began to enter the deepest part of me, to set off small explosions in my brain.

"No!" I heard myself yelling. "What you're saying

143

isn't true at all. It's all wrong." I jumped down from the examining table, clutching the covering sheet with one hand and holding the paper johnny closed with the other. I was screaming in her face, but I didn't care. "What kind of doctor are you anyway? How could you miss something so obvious? I'm having a baby. A very holy baby. I am! All the signs can't be wrong."

She tried to steady me with her hand on my arm, but I shook it free. She kept her own voice low and matter-of-fact.

"At the beginning you can get a false negative result. But if you're as far along as you seem to think, there would be significant changes in your body. We'd be able to feel and hear the baby. There'd be no doubt about it."

"You're wrong. You're dead *wrong!*" I yelled again. Already, questions were lining up inside my head like wiggly kids waiting for a roller coaster ride.

"What about how sick I felt at the beginning, just like my grandmother's secretary? What about the weight I gained, the way I'm always sleepy like Madeline's sister was? Explain *that!* And what about the fast little heartbeat? Huh? What about that?"

"A false pregnancy," she said as if it were an absolute fact. "Even if you were pregnant, dear," she said, "no one would be able to hear the heartbeat, not even the mother, without a stethoscope or fetal monitor."

And then she said something about how there have been countless cases where if someone believes strongly enough that they've conceived, their body "goes through many of the changes we normally associate with a fecund state." She said how she knew I wasn't faking it or anything and that I really was experiencing "the bodily changes associated with childbearing." She got so clinical at this point that she lost me until she said how fathers have even been known to have labor pains along with their wives and something like, "Suggestion is a powerful tool, Taswell. You've used it with great imagination, though I can't understand why. Perhaps you and Sister Francesca can sort this out."

"Thank goodness there wasn't some boy involved," said Sister Eduard after she'd bustled in and demanded to know the results of Dr. Philips's examination, "that she is still undefiled."

"A mother of a prophet has to be undefiled!" I stated.

"Saints preserve us!" she said then. "You don't still believe in this Virgin birth thing? You can't be holding onto that bizarre story in view of all that Dr. Philips has just told you!"

"Oh, ye of little faith," I said.

Sister Eduard put two fingers on each temple and thumped them up and down as if she was trying to clear her mind. Then she looked directly at me.

"Snap out of this at once, do you hear? You must

come to your senses immediately and abandon this foolish charade."

"I've seen signs and wonders," I proclaimed in the strongest voice I could muster under the circumstances.

"Pul*eeze!* Too many movies is more like what you've seen! I will not listen to any more of this foolishness."

She crossed herself while staring straight at me, and she genuflected in the doorway on her way out as if to guard against overpowering evil and keep it contained.

They are ripping at *my* heart, Pim. They are tearing it out in pieces. But I'll find a way to stop them. Even if Grace never believed me, I know Madeline still does.

Your person,

Taswell

Thursday, April 22

Dear Taswell,

I'm not supposed to be talking to you. But writing is different, isn't it?

They say you aren't pregnant at all. I don't understand. Did you trick the doctor or what? Can somebody do that? Well, I guess you could. You're not like anyone else.

I want to help you with your mission, but I don't know how. In that room, with both of us being questioned like that by Sister Francesca and Grace, it seemed as if we were in this together. It's not easy to stop believing in something inspired. I mean, I think you must have been inspired. I think I was, too. For sure.

But what do we do now?

Your friend,

Madeline

Dear Madeline,

We pray hard. Really, really hard. And wait for guidance.

Fear not!

Your friend,

Taswell

Dear Taswell,

Sister Eduard called this afternoon and insisted that I come there at once. She would not tell me anything at all except to imply that your therapy is not going well and Sister Francesca and I need to talk. This couldn't come at a more inconvenient time for me as we are launching a new series tomorrow and I need to be in Chicago by the end of the week. Really, Taswell. I wish you would give some thought to the timing of your outbursts or whatever it is that is upsetting Sister Eduard.

I told her that I could not get away before Monday,

and she finally had to accept that, though she hinted at calling Charles if I didn't make myself available. Charles will be there soon enough, but only, I hope, after we've settled this unfortunate matter. It would only confirm his original objection to Our Lady's.

You are fourteen years old, Taswell. It's time you considered the priorities of persons other than yourself.

Fondly,
Mavis

Dear Mavis,

I'm glad I'll be seeing you on Monday and that Sister Eduard didn't tell you anything yet. I think you will be very surprised and maybe amazed. I have been praying that you will understand. It's not something terrible, as you seem to think. In fact, it's something really wonderful. It's just that some people around here are a little mixed up.

Please keep an open mind.

Your loving granddaughter,
Taswell

Friday, April 23

Dear Pim,

Since Wednesday I've been temporarily excused from classes. I think it's supposed to be a punishment, but it's just what I wanted. They wouldn't let me stay in chapel as I proposed, so I've been in my room all day. Grace brought me chicken soup at lunch, though I'm not very hungry anymore. It's sort of weird, after always feeling starved. I don't know what the other girls have been told.

I can't imagine ever leaving this room. The part of the sky I can see through the pines keeps changing from one murky color to another. It's orangey mud now with clouds speeding up like bubbles in water that's about to boil. It's like they're getting ready for something. Like maybe there'll be a sign in the clouds. Please, Pim. Please put one there.

Your person,
Taswell

Saturday, April 24

Dear Taswell,

My sister sent me an article from the Sunday paper called "Children Raising Children." It's all about teenagers having babies and how hard it is to raise them. She's been sending me stuff like that ever since she discovered how incredibly exhausted she is raising her own babies. Did you know a baby goes through like twenty-five diapers a day and spits up all over the whole house and everyone in it and hardly ever sleeps? They never stop eating either.

Sometimes I think my parents sent me here because they thought I was too interested in boys. I guess I am, but I'm not dumb enough to get pregnant. I don't mean that *you're* dumb. I know you couldn't help it and are special and everything.

But the article made me think how you're going to have to take care of this kid once it gets here. Have you ever thought about that? Do you have a plan? Maybe we should be working on one—where you'll live and how you'll pay for everything and how you're going to get some sleep. All kinds of stuff like that. Let me know when you're coming out of your room so we can talk about this. It's real important!

Your friend,
Madeline

Saturday, April 24

Dear Madeline,

I didn't know that babies were *that* much trouble. They look so peaceful and quiet in pictures. I haven't known many. And I guess I sort of thought that since God wants to give me this baby, He's going to provide for it. It would be nice to have a kind of protector like Joseph was for Mary, but that doesn't seem to be working out. If you hear anything at all about Grace's brother Simon leaving the seminary, let me know right away. I guess we should talk, though. Maybe after my grandmother gets here Monday and I know if I'm going to be expelled or what.

Your friend,
Taswell

Saturday, April 24

Dear Taswell,

I can't believe you're being so laid back about this! Didn't you ever hear how God helps those who help themselves? I mean, how easy did He make it for Mary? She had to have her baby in a dingy old stable with a bunch of smelly animals.

We need a plan. And soon.

Your friend,
Madeline

Monday, April 26

Dear Pim,

Madeline is suddenly getting all bent out of shape again. It must be part of the difficult role she's being asked to play, so I guess I'd better listen. I sent her a note to meet me tonight after vespers.

Today Mavis was sitting in the waiting room of the

office when they led me in like some prisoner. She was perched on one of those useless damask chairs the color of rotten cherries and not big enough to fit anybody's bottom. She got up, slowly, reaching out to hold me at arm's length as if I had a disease.

"You look terrible!" she said, with her lips turned down in such a look of disgust that it made me think for the first time in three or four days how I must appear. I haven't washed my hair in a while, hardly even combed it, though Grace insisted I brush my teeth before she'd let me out of my room. My cardigan has some stains on the front. I can't wash it because it's the only one I have that's big enough.

Mavis led me at arm's length to the chair beside her before venturing close enough to whisper, "Now, Taswell. What is all this about? Why all this secrecy? Why in the world are you so unbelievably unkempt? Sister Eduard has told me nothing."

"That's a relief," I said, "because they have it all wrong."

"They?"

"All the nuns. Everyone but Madeline."

"The little girl you've been bullying."

"I haven't been bullying anyone," I shouted. "I told you. They have it all wrong."

"Let's be very calm and quiet," she said then. "Let's not become ruffled. I'm sure we can discuss this, whatever it is, without becoming emotionally overwrought."

I tried. I was absolutely quiet and then spoke very very slowly. But as soon as I told her about the baby, she turned pale green. I swear it—from under the eyes right down to her pink collar. And it wasn't long before she was the one shouting.

"A virgin birth! Are you crazy? Do you think I know nothing? What in the world are you trying to pull?"

"I'm not trying to pull anything," I said. "You were going to keep an open mind. You were going to listen to me."

"No, Taswell. That was your request. But it's quite impossible, given this kind of information. A prophet for the New Millennium! Indeed!"

Grace rushed back in as if she'd been waiting by the door. She asked if Mavis wanted to see Sister Eduard now.

"Right now!" she said. "Immediately. She should have warned me about this bizarre situation herself and not made it into some vague mystery. There is nothing vague or mysterious here. Taswell is either pregnant by conventional means or she is not. She is either genuinely and seriously disturbed or she is a charlatan. Look at her. Just look at her!"

"You are upset," said Grace.

"Upset!" She paused. "I am not upset. I am livid! I

am irate! I am horrified!" Her eyes traveled wildly around the room while avoiding mine altogether.

It was only seconds before Sister Eduard came running, her skirts pulled up and her habit flying. She dashed through the girls mulling around in the hall and came to a halt at Mavis's feet like a duck skidding onto the surface of a lake on its tail feathers. She nodded, took Mavis's elbow and my hand, then pushed and pulled us into her office and shut the door.

"I should have been present," she said. "I thought it might be better if Taswell spoke with you first, but clearly, that was a mistake. I apologize. I heartily apologize."

"I only want to know the facts. I want to know them before I remove Taswell from this school and from your obvious lack of supervision. I mistakenly assumed she would be protected here."

"Oh, it's not what you think. Goodness, it's nothing like what you must be thinking. Taswell has been examined by a reputable gynecologist, and she isn't even a little bit pregnant," said Sister Eduard. She beamed with good cheer.

"I was never sure what that meant," said Mavis. "You are either pregnant or you are not. And if Taswell is not, then she is completely and utterly delusional."

"That is our little problem," said Sister Eduard as if she had just stepped under some dark cloud. "She refuses to give up the fantasy. She believes herself to be singled out."

"I have been," I said.

"You have certainly not been," declared Mavis. Then she looked as if she'd just made a clever discovery. "But you might very well be hatching some devious little plan." She turned to Sister Eduard. "She is full of devious little plans."

"We are aware of that," said Sister. "All the more reason why we felt you should hear this from her own lips. That," and here her face got puffy and I thought she was going to cry, "and the fact that I truly didn't know how to tell you over the phone."

I had thought Mavis would try to understand. I knew it would be hard for her, but I thought she'd at least try. Had she listened to my mother? Did she try to help her? I always thought she must have. Is that the reason my mother ran away?

But neither Sister nor Mavis would listen to me, to my side.

Mavis kept threatening to take me out of school immediately, but Sister Eduard finally convinced her to let me finish out the term. She said Sister Francesca thought she was having some success at last (success at what, I wondered) and said that classes are over at the end of May anyway.

"Don't make up your mind until you've spoken

with Sister Francesca," Sister Eduard said to Mavis. "I'm sure she can help you understand the situation." Then she hurried her away, leaving me to sit by myself on one of those uncomfortable chairs for another hour.

When Mavis came back alone, she spoke to me as if I were either sick or breakable. And she made a point of telling me in a very reasonable tone of voice that she and Wilfred will not be coming to Parents' Weekend so that I'll have time alone with Charles. She said to think long and hard about what I'm claiming. To try to separate fact from fantasy. To think of Sister Francesca as my friend.

Then she sort of lurched forward, and I was startled to think that she was going to hug me. But, of course, she didn't. She blew a kiss from the door, though, and I automatically blew one back, the same way I've always done every time she's left me behind for something more important.

"Dad" will be here in a few days. I wonder if Mavis will tell him anything. Maybe he'll listen to me. Maybe. Though I doubt it.

The Angelus is ringing. At night like this, it makes the wolves howl.

My soul doth magnify the Lord
And my spirit rejoices in God my Saviour

For he has regarded the humility of His handmaiden.

I'm His handmaiden, too. I am. And I refuse to be afraid.
  Your person,
  Taswell

FIFTEEN

———◆———

Dear Pim,

I am back in classes this week. Since I have to live here and eat in the refectory with everyone, I've decided to carry on as if things are the same as ever. I was prepared to offer it all up as a penance, but it really hasn't been so bad. It's not as if I haven't had some experience with people avoiding me. A lot of the girls do treat me as if I have something catching. They act like Madeline is really brave to be seen with me. And I've had to double up on sessions with Sister Francesca. People notice things like that.

There was hardly anyone in study hall last night. With only the bright lights in front turned on, Madeline and I sat in desks at the back with our books open in front of us. We kept our voices low. At least I kept my voice low. Sister Bruno would wander out from the kitchen and look in at us whenever Madeline forgot.

As soon as Madeline sat down, she started harping on how am I going to take care of the baby, like that in itself is going to require a major miracle. I had to admit that I haven't thought much about it. I guess I figured Mavis would step in, the way she did to take care of me, though *I* would never run away or anything. Now, of course, I realize that was never a realistic hope.

"Face it," Madeline said finally. "You thought everyone would feel so honored about her being a prophet and all, that the baby could just stay here, in your own room maybe, and be fussed over by all the nuns and you could keep going to school."

I just couldn't tell her that I hadn't exactly thought that far ahead. (The idea of all the nuns fluttering around the bassinet like those fairies in the Sleeping Beauty ballet was really very appealing, though.) And I had sort of assumed that I could keep going to school. I still don't see why that should be a problem. I mean, it's just one baby. How much trouble can one divinely inspired baby be? She's bound to be super good and everything.

"How do you know that?" Madeline asked. "A baby's a baby. When I was home at Easter, my sister's babies kept everyone awake. They never ever shut up.

And somebody had to hold them or push them around or feed them twenty-four hours a day. It drove me right out of the house whenever they pooped. Yuck! I couldn't wait to get back here. You know it can't be normal to get homesick for this place!"

"I think you're making some of this up."

"Look," she said, so loudly that Sister Bruno appeared in the doorway again and frowned, "I finally had to believe you, didn't I? Well, you're just going to have to believe me. This baby, any baby, needs somebody to run around all day and all night and take care of it."

She stopped talking for a long time as if the very thought of all that baby care had worn her out.

"Maybe this isn't such a good idea," she said at last.

"What do you mean?" I asked. "What can you possibly mean by that? It's going to happen. There's nothing we can do about it, even if we wanted to."

"Well, what if God's trying to tell us something. What if he's trying to say that He's changed his mind?"

"He can't change his mind," I said. "Not now. Not after we've both been inspired and I've been more or less overshadowed and everything."

"I thought God could do anything."

"It sounds like that old trick question," I said. "Can God make a rock so big He can't lift it?"

"Can He?"

"Forget it!"

"I really want to know."

"Everyone wants to know. That's why it's a trick question."

"Well," she said, moving closer and twisting the moon and star charm on her neck chain until I thought she was going to pull it off or choke herself, "maybe you've been getting His messages all wrong. Maybe they didn't ever mean what you thought they did."

She stopped talking again and just kind of stared into space.

Then she suddenly said, "I think the message at this very minute is pretty clear," and she jumped up as though she was going to leave. "This baby thing. It's not a very good idea."

I panicked. "Does that mean you're not going to help me?"

"I'll help you," she said. "I'm trying to help you right now."

But then she picked up her stuff and left without explaining. What do you think she meant, Pim?

You know what's the worst? It's how silent *you* are. I'm like drowning in your silence. And now it looks as if Madeline wants me to wake up some morning and say it was all a dream or something. I can't do it, Pim. I won't.

Your person,
Taswell

Dear Mavis,

I didn't think you would feel the way you do about this. I guess I didn't think about how you'd feel and I'm sorry for that.

It's important that you know I'm not trying to trick anyone, though. I would never try to trick you, especially.

You'll be happy that I seem to have lost my appetite at last.

Your loving granddaughter,
Taswell

Dear Madeline,

Just so I'm sure, the other night did you mean that you'll still be my friend no matter what? That you'll help me, even though you're having doubts? Grace told me once that having faith doesn't mean you don't have any doubts, that doubts are natural and necessary. I have some, too, sometimes.

Your friend,
Taswell

Dear Taswell,

Maybe you really should be a nun. Maybe that's what this is all about. You sure do sound like one sometimes.

And yes, I'll still be your friend, no matter what. Though I don't like it much when you get preachy.

I think you should know that I had another dream about you, but this time you were really skinny again and you had a boyfriend. (It wasn't Simon.) And it didn't look to me like there was a baby anywhere in sight. No babies anywhere.

Your friend,
Madeline

Dear Pim

I can't hear the heartbeat anymore. It scares me.

The sessions with Sister Francesca have been like the earlier silent ones. I just don't have anything to say to her. Maybe you've noticed how she incessantly picks at her lower lip lately. I hope I'm not driving her insane.

This morning I went to high mass at six o'clock with the nuns. It's really quiet at that hour and so comforting to hear their voices chanting the responses together. I prayed and prayed for guidance, and just as the light from the rose window hit the chalice, it came to me. I should fast. That's what I need to do. Fast until I'm given some direction, like the saints did, like even Jesus did in the desert. I don't know why I never thought of it before. Since I'm not very hungry anymore anyway, it seems like a really good idea. I think I'll wait, though, until after breakfast, because, as you probably know, Sister Bruno makes these really delicious apple pancakes on Saturdays.

Your person,
Taswell

Saturday, May 1

Dear Pim,

I had completely forgotten that this is Parents' Weekend and didn't wake up to the fact until breakfast when I noticed how everyone had on clean jeans or regular dresses and jewelry and eye makeup.

With parents supposed to be arriving any time, I hurried back to my room and unburied the loose dress with little violet flowers I'd worn the first day here. Because it has no waist, it still fit okay. But when Grace knocked and said that Charles was waiting in the parlor, I felt so grungy and rumpled, like maybe I should pretend to be sick or maybe I should disappear into the woods for a few days. I knew I wouldn't get away with either one with Grace standing there, so I let her arrange my hair into a kind of twist that made me look all eyes. She even put my glasses back on my face and stuck around until I started down the stairs. Though I wasn't intending to, I seemed to be taking them in painfully slow motion. Other girls were passing me like racehorses.

Sometimes, you know, people's feelings seem to be outside of themselves. Did you know that? Sometimes, a person can't even decide what the feelings are. They, the feelings, just sort of float out there, hover around, and wait. That's what it was like when I walked into the parlor and saw Monique. I hadn't even noticed Charles, yet, over by the window. But Monique was waiting for me, waiting to scoop me up and press me against her enormous roundness as if I were some giant rag doll. Up against the big warm balloon of her, I could hardly breathe but just held on while I tried to catch some of those stupid feelings floating around. Why was she here? What did it mean? How *did* I feel about it? She held me away from her then, not like I was fragile or offensive, but like she wanted to have a better look at me, like she wanted someplace to put her enormous grin.

"I couldn't help myself," she said then. "I know I was invited to stay home, but I wanted to see you, to see what this place is like and to find out why Mavis is so upset. You seem perfectly fine to me. More than fine. You look great."

Did I really? Could I possibly look okay after all? Great even? It was hard to believe.

"Hey! You've put on a little weight. Not too surprising your first year away at boarding school."

The old Freshman disease thing. I guess she didn't know, that Mavis hadn't told her. It meant that Charles probably didn't know either. It meant that I would have to tell him myself.

The rest of the day was pretty confusing. I'll write about it tomorrow when I decide what it all means.

Your person,

Taswell

SIXTEEN

Sunday, May 2

Dear Pim,

The first thing I noticed, the first major thing, was how different Monique looks from me. I mean I can't begin to measure up to Monique's Tweedle Dee look — this great round middle balancing above feet I'm sure she can't even see when she's standing up.

"Wow," said Madeline when she met her. "You look like my sister did at the very end!"

"The very end of what?" Monique wanted to know.

"Oh, just before she delivered. You know. Right before."

"It's close," said Charles. He came up behind her and held her with both arms. "But she wanted to see Taswell. I couldn't talk her out of it."

For a second or so I wished that Charles and I knew how to touch each other. Neither one of us has ever figured it out, or even made a stab at it. I watched other girls run up to their fathers and give them big smacking kisses and I wondered how they did that—if it was hard at first, if it was something you could learn.

Charles sort of patted my shoulder, but it was Monique who took my hand, and said, "Lead away. I want to see this dungeon for young women. Spare me nothing—the rack, the chastity belts, the isolation pits."

"It's not like that," I said. "Though the walls are kind of cold and clammy and they turn gaslights on in the halls at night to keep down the electric bill. Otherwise it's just your average phony castle on a remote mountaintop surrounded by wolves and inhabited by religious zealots."

She laughed right out loud, then, with this rolling kind of chuckle. And Charles did too, his own bumpy laugh. It made me think that maybe we were sounding like a real family. Like maybe it looked as if I were showing my real family around just the way that Madeline was.

After I'd taken them to the classrooms, gym, and chapel and we'd come to my own room (which I'd cleaned up, sort of—at least I'd hung up most of the clothes), Monique said how she and I had some girl-talking to do and we'd meet Charles a little later in the parlor for coffee. I could tell from the way he cupped my chin with his hand for a minute and then just turned and trotted off down the hall with a little wave, that he'd been expecting this, and it was so clear all of a sudden that it was some kind of setup. I felt stupid and naive. I'd been playing right along with their plan, whatever it was. Charles must be aware of everything after all. He'd brought Monique along, because he didn't know how to talk to me about it. It wasn't because she was just dying to see me. What a dope I was!

"I don't know what we have to talk about," I said, and I could feel my words turning into little blocks of ice as they hit the air.

"What's the matter?" said Monique. "We were getting along so well. It felt so good."

"I don't know what you mean," I said.

"Yes, you do. Of course you do. We were talking together like friends, like family."

"Friends don't try to manipulate you," I flung at her.

"No," she said, "but they do try to help each other. That's what I'm here for. That's why I came. It would have been a whole lot more comfortable, and probably safer, to have stayed at home."

She slowly lowered herself into the empty chair, placing one hand on the small of her back. She gave a little gasp when she'd finally landed.

"Imagine what it was like trying to buckle up on the plane!"

She smiled. There's something about her smile. It has a kind of life of its own. It was all I could do not to smile back.

"Oops!" she said, wincing. "It must be doing another lay-up. This is definitely a basketball player. Here feel this," and she reached for my hand and held it against her. I felt a firm thrust against my open palm.

"Does it do that all the time?" I asked.

"Oh, not every single minute, thank heaven. But enough to make me feel like a punching bag sometimes."

"Mine doesn't. At least not that much," I said without thinking. I was just so amazed. But she didn't act surprised.

"Your baby?"

"Yes," I said. "Maybe my baby sleeps more than yours."

"All babies are different," she said.

"They told you," I said.

"Well," she answered, "they told Charles and, of course, he told me."

Of course!

"And I thought how it must feel pretty wonderful to be singled out like that, to be such an important person in God's plan. I thought how you would have to be very brave to agree to all the things that could follow."

"I guess," I said. What was she getting at?

"It's just such an awesome experience to be carrying a baby at all. This little new life. I can't imagine what it must be like to carry a messenger of God."

"You don't believe me," I said then. "No one does, you know. So don't pretend."

"I want to believe you. I know that *you* are convinced. And if you are, you must have very good reasons for believing that you've been singled out, for believing in this 'prophet.' Isn't that what you call her?"

"I call her Aileen," I said. "Bearer of the Light."

"A very appropriate name for a prophet. It's your mother's name, too, isn't it?"

"Yes," I said.

"Well. Now you're not going to believe me. But when Charles told me about it, I said how I wanted to reserve judgment until I'd seen you, that you were really a very noble young woman, and this was just the kind of thing that might happen to you, to someone with your very high ideals. I said I was sure that if God did want to create a prophet for the New Millennium, you'd be just the kind of person He would choose to be her mother. A little too young maybe, but certainly the right type of person."

"You're right about one thing," I said. "I don't believe you."

"Well, it's true," she said. "But now that I've seen you, I think your doctor must be right."

"How can you possibly tell? How can you tell just like that?"

"For starters, you don't have that glow about you that many expectant women get—that bloom that would surely show itself in the mother of someone so holy."

What was she talking about?

"And you're not the size of someone planning to deliver in a month or two. Look at me!"

I had been looking at her. I hadn't been able to take my eyes off her since she arrived. She was so...so ripe, like a fruit tree in the middle of summer, like...yes, like she was in bloom or something.

"Also, you say your baby doesn't kick, doesn't move around all that much."

"And you said all babies are different."

"It's true. But with any baby, you'd feel life some times, more and more with the growth of the fetus. At some point you'd know for certain that there was a living, growing being inside of you. Do you in fact know this for certain?"

"Yes. For certain," I said.

"No doubts at all? No feelings that you might be mistaken? Anyone would understand if you decide that you are."

"No, they wouldn't," I said. "They'd think I'm crazy. I mean really crazy."

"I wouldn't think that."

"Well, Charles would," I told her. "And Mavis. She thinks I'm trying to trick her." I couldn't breathe. I was like choking without making any sound.

"Please," I said. When I could finally speak, tears were coming fast and turning the flowers on my dress into dark purple stains. "Just go away."

But she didn't move.

"Is that what you want? What you really want?"

What did I want? I wanted something so backward I could hardly believe it. I wanted her to have a lap that I could throw myself into, could curl up in, collapse in. She was talking to me as no one else ever had. She was trying, really trying to get inside my head, to understand my feelings, to know what I thought, what I wanted, what I believed. It was so overwhelming, so irresistible. She not only looked like a mother, she was being a mother, *my* mother, the mother I had always wanted so badly.

She pushed herself up with both hands until she was standing right in front of me. But she didn't move any closer, and her two arms rested on top of her stomach.

"I'll go find Charles. I didn't mean to upset you. I think your desire for a baby to love is very normal and natural. Many girls your age have it. You've just been a bit more inventive about it than most."

"You're just saying that. You think I'm crazy, too," I said.

"No," she said. "I don't at all. I do think you want someone to love completely. Just as we all do." She smoothed her dress down to her hips with her two hands. "Maybe this child—your sister or brother—will be lucky enough to get some of that love. And you're correct about the world needing prophets. With your unique way of looking at things, you'd probably make a good one yourself."

What she was saying was turning me inside out. It was causing me to look too closely at places I thought were hidden away, letting other things that didn't seem to fit anywhere slip away. It was making me feel as if I'd been existing in some kind of whirling machine that had been spinning faster and faster and wouldn't let me leave, that I'd flown from it at last, like a glob of paint from a centrifuge, that I'd landed on my own two feet.

When she started to leave and I cautiously reached out to put my arm around her, she didn't seem nearly as surprised as I was.

Your person,
Taswell

Thursday, May 6

Dear Pim,

These past few days, I've had lots more time to think about it all, how I may have manufactured you because I needed to and how you didn't really let me down because you probably didn't ever exist. But at times it seems like it was more what Madeline said, that you were there all right, and the signs were there, too, but I was reading them all wrong.

When you've believed in things, in important things, for such a long time, when you've counted on them, it's really hard to just let go. It's like making this great leap across a precipice, like leaving little pieces of yourself on the other side and never being able to leap back and collect them. It's like not really knowing who you are anymore, of having to learn about this whole new person that you've suddenly become.

Can you believe it? It was Charles who finally explained things to Mavis, how I hadn't become this devious out-of-control teenager that she'd always feared I would. And of course, it was Monique who had explained things to Charles. So everything seems to be turning out all right.

What do you think? But then, I guess I'll never know what you think or even if you think. It's just another mystery. Grace says you bite off a whole bunch of those when you decide to believe in anything. I'm okay with that. What I do have a problem with, though, are those clear memories of you all those years ago—the green suit, the glassy skin, your voice like a silver flute. Now, when I picture you in my mind, you have these amazing golden wings too. They're very tightly woven and awfully bright. I hope that's what you wanted. And I hope you'll understand that I won't be writing to you anymore. Well, maybe a letter once in awhile. From Paris. Or from wherever my family happens to be at the time.

Your person,
Taswell

Dear Daniel,

Congratulations on being born. I wanted to be the very first to tell you that. You kicked my hand, you know, when we were still thinking you were going to be some basketball player. Well, maybe you will be. There are lots of things that you can be in this world. And there will be lots of time to learn about them. Right now, you still have to learn to do important things like smile and talk and walk.

I'm going to be there to help you with all the stuff that comes after that. And just in case you notice some spirit hanging around to protect you, I'll believe it and everything, but I'll stick around, too, just in case.

Your sister,
Taswell